DEATH CO...

DEATH

COMES TO

Machu Picchu

THOMAS M. DANIEL

2019 · FITHIAN PRESS, MCKINLEYVILLE, CALIFORNIA

Published by Fithian Press
A division of Daniel and Daniel, Publishers, Inc.
Post Office Box 2790
McKinleyville, CA 95519
www.danielpublishing.com

Distributed by SCB Distributors (800) 729-6423

Cover image: Tatsuya Ohinata/iStock photo

LIBRARY OF CONGRESS CATALOGING-IN-PUBLICATION DATA
Names: Daniel, Thomas M., [date] author.
Title: Death comes to Machu Picchu / by Thomas M. Daniel.
Description: McKinleyville, California : Fithian Press, 2019. | Summary:
"Ten tourists find themselves spending the night of Christmas Eve together at the
    inn associated with the Machu Picchu ruins, high in the Peruvian Andes. They are
    cut off by weather from the world below, and they spend the afternoon getting to
    know each other. There are two lone men in the group, but most of the rest are
    couples-husbands and wives and a mother with her adult daughter. These tourists
    come from different walks of life; one man is a travel agent, another man works for
    the CIA, a Swedish couple work for the United States Embassy, an unmarried young
    twosome are university students, and so on. They are different from one another,
    except for one characteristic that each keeps secret from the others: They are all in
    denial about their dependency on cocaine and their intention to smuggle a small
    supply of the drug out of Peru"— Provided by publisher.
Identifiers: LCCN 2019036187 | ISBN 9781564746207 (trade paperback)
Subjects: LCSH: Drug traffic—Peru—Fiction.
Classification: LCC PS3604.A5256 D43 2019 | DDC 813/.6—dc23
LC record available at https://lccn.loc.gov/2019036187

Contents

DEATH COMES TO MACHU PICCHU

Prologue

TED'S OFFICE DOOR BURST OPEN. Charles pushed his way in, carrying a pistol in his right hand.

"I tried to stop him," Ted's secretary, Gloria, said. "But he just pushed ahead. And he has a gun."

"That's all right, Gloria. Go back and call 911." She turned back toward her desk to reach the telephone.

Charles pushed the office door closed. "You remember me, don't you, Ted. "I'm the guy you sent to prison for a murder I didn't commit—a murder you committed. And now I'm out, and I'm ready to settle my score with you. Twenty years in a Peruvian prison. I've had lots of time to anticipate this moment. I'm going to kill you."

CHAPTER ONE

Ted and Charles

THE LAN BOEING 737 came to a stop at a gate at the Lima terminal. Ted Hewes retrieved his brief case from the overhead rack and tucked his laptop PC into it. Exiting the plane, he joined the crowd of travel-weary people flowing from the several overnight flights that had landed at about the same time and made his way to the Peru customs area. After enduring a long and slowly moving line, he presented his passport and retrieved his checked luggage. Dodging taxis, he crossed the airport drive to the Wyndham Hotel where he had reserved a room. At the hotel's check-in desk, he presented his credit card. He had paid for the prior night when he made the reservation, so that the room would be available to him this morning.

Ted's divorce from Cynthia had brought out the worst in both of them, he thought. Their marriage had been intermittently shaky from its start, but that situation was minor when considered against the acrimony of the divorce proceedings. And their two children had been unfortunately victimized by their parents' bitter squabbling. Cynthia's mother had stepped into the situation and provided the children the love and devotion that were somehow displaced from the parents by their unhappy fight.

Ted and Cynthia had lived comfortably. They were not rich, neither in his mind nor in hers. Yet there was little that they wanted that they could not afford—or somehow stretch their budget to accommodate. They had two cars. Cynthia drove a Lexus. He drove a Jeep Wrangler. The two vehicles suited their individual self images. Cynthia's Lexus connoted social status to her. Ted's Wrangler made him feel apart and somehow superior to their neighbors.

They belonged to the local country club. He played an occasional round of golf. He was not good at the game, agreeing perhaps with Mark Twain's assessment that a round of golf was "a good walk spoiled." However, golf at the club often provided important business contacts for him. He hosted clients for golf and for drinks and often a meal following eighteen holes. He made the club membership and the entertainment expenses a business expense on Schedule C of his 1040 tax return. He kept careful records for his accountant, detailing business items discussed at these outings. These accounts were not infrequently embellished; no one expected complete honesty when dealing with the IRS, he believed.

Cynthia was a good tennis player. She had a strong serve with a spin that produced an unexpectedly low and angled bounce. She could place her serve wherever she chose. Her returns from either the back court or the net were equally devilish for her opponents. The club kept ladder ranking its tennis-playing members. While not at the top, Cynthia was not far from it. She felt that being recognized as a good tennis player was important for their standing in the community—or at least that standing in the community to which she and Ted aspired.

She took lessons from the club "pro," a young man whose attention flattered her. She recognized that his flattery was not unique to her and was part of the persona he assumed to make himself appreciated at the club. Nevertheless, she liked it. She longed for flattery; it seldom came from Ted, although it had in earlier days of their marriage.

The kids were learning to swim in the club pool. Water safety was important for growing children, Cynthia believed. They enjoyed their pool time, if not the lessons themselves. Moreover, swimming kept them occupied while the parents pursued their club agendas.

Cynthia was an aspiring poet hoping to be recognized. She had managed to place one of her poems in *The New Yorker*, and she considered that a major victory, a major justification. A first that would be followed by others, she hoped. A start in the literary world. She looked upon herself as a neophyte Sylvia Plath. Plath, her private role model, had started writing poetry while a student at Smith College. Cynthia had done the same while a student at Vassar. Unlike Plath, however, she failed to achieve literary recognition while a student. Her current success with *The New Yorker* brought redemption in her mind. Well deserved, she felt. Ted ignored, sometimes seeming to brush aside, her creative efforts. That disappointed her. It would not have happened earlier in their life together.

Ted had grown up in Corning, New York. He was an only child. His father was a hot shop worker shaping glass in the Corning Glass Works. He was skilled, and proud of his accomplishments. His mother also worked at the Glass Works. She was a reception clerk at the visitors' desk. They were a close-knit, if small family. A loving family, Ted knew.

An average student but a good athlete, Ted played half-back on his high school football team. He liked the sanctioned roughness of football. His parents regularly attended the school's games to watch him play. They discussed and reviewed those events at dinners on nights following games, usually with flattering assessments of his performance.

Ted often thought that those high school fall semesters were the happiest days of his life. It was those years, Ted believed, when he had moved from boyhood to manhood. After a homecoming dance during his senior year, he tried to seduce his date. She was widely recognized as the prettiest girl—young woman—in the senior class. Others must have asked her to the dance and been refused, he thought. He supposed sex with one's date was part of homecoming week, and was much chagrined when she rebuffed him. He boasted to friends that he had succeeded, however.

He enrolled in SUNY (State University of New York) in New Paltz, leaving home for that Hudson River campus and town. He majored in finance and enjoyed the accounting courses that some of his classmates found tedious. He was a good student. A few B's, but mostly A grades. A better academic record than he had achieved in high school. His SUNY classes stimulated him in a way that his high school subjects had never done. They were more interesting and seemed more relevant to what he hoped his future career would be.

Social life at the university centered on fraternities, and Ted joined Alpha Delta Phi. He drank too much at fraternity parties on some weekends, especially after football or basketball games. He did not feel guilty about this; it was normal college life, he believed.

Ted found himself liking not only the college but also the surrounding town of New Paltz. He hiked and climbed rock cliffs in the Shawangunk Mountains west of New Paltz. Climbing those rock faces was not easy. He enjoyed the challenge, however, and made many return trips to them, gradually becoming proficient, perhaps expert, at scaling them.

To his surprise, he found he enjoyed wandering through and visiting the historic old Huguenot town of New Paltz. The old houses fascinated him. He was intrigued to note that many of them were solidly built of stone, designed to serve as defensive bastions with ports for defending rifles.

Following college he felt aimless, not knowing what he wanted to do. Impulsively and without carefully considering the matter, Ted joined the Peace Corps. He was welcomed as what the agency called a "BA Generalist." Not possessing specific skills, he would be trained in language and in techniques to facilitate his entry into an indigenous community as well as matters relevant to his particular upcoming role. Soon he found himself at a training site in Costa Rica, learning Spanish and more about growing potatoes than he thought anyone needed to know. He then spent three years in a small Bolivian town in the intermountain Altiplano demonstrating the virtues of hybrid potatoes to the local farmers. He was provided with a motorcycle to facilitate travel between the separate farms where he would introduce the potatoes. When he returned at the completion of his tour, the bike would remain behind.

Ted returned to Corning and found a job in a local bank. One year later he met Cynthia. Five years younger than Ted, she had returned from Vassar during the summer after her sophomore year and found a position filling in for vacationing tellers at the bank where Ted worked. She flirted with him, and soon they were dating—with increasing frequency. When she returned to Vassar, Ted drove to Poughkeepsie on many weekends.

After a year in Corning, Ted moved to New York City. Two days before boarding a train for New York, Ted asked Cynthia to marry him. Two weeks after Cynthia's graduation from Vassar, they were married in Corning surrounded by friends and family. A good couple, a good marriage, their family and friends thought. In fact, they were and it was. They moved into a crowded, one-bedroom Manhattan apartment in a neighborhood west of Columbus Circle and the Museum of Modern Art. Cynthia found a job at the reception desk of the museum.

Ted worked long hours at a brokerage in lower Manhattan, trying to sell stocks to New York City and Corning friends, neighbors, anyone who might like to invest savings in what he felt was a much sounder venue than a bank; inflation would devalue money sequestered in a bank savings account. Ted followed the financial world closely, and he was sure he could give his clients excellent advice and offer them hard-to-recognize opportunities. He built a substantial stock portfolio for himself. About half of his holdings were ones that he and his stock broker colleagues called "Steady Eddies." Dependable stocks in large capital corporations. They increased in value at reasonably predictable if modest rates. The other half were invested in what the industry called "growth stocks." Some caution buttressed by careful research was needed to succeed with these holdings, and he had successfully applied both research and caution to selecting his holdings. And he had done well. He had purchased shares in Apple Computers when they were first issued and watched their value soar.

Increasingly prosperous and now parents, Ted and Cynthia moved to Greenwich, Connecticut. This meant a daily commute for Ted, during which he devoted himself to financial research on his laptop computer and the day's edition of *The Wall Street Journal*. Time well spent, he felt. For Cynthia, the move thrust her into the role of suburban parent, a life she accepted and enjoyed.

Neither Cynthia nor Ted was ready to devote the energy needed in a marriage to make theirs successful. While in New York, they seldom went out—restaurant meals seemed beyond their budget—and they spent most of their evenings in their apartment watching television. They did not partake of the many opportunities for intellectual stimulation afforded by New York City. After moving from the city to suburban Connecticut, their lives became increasingly separate. Ted's commute added to their separation. Cynthia's life focused on the children and their activities and also on country club-centered recreation and socialization. Thinking back, Ted decided their lives together had simply "run out of steam."

The marriage was over now. Ted was free, if a good bit poorer, and he had booked this trip to South America to help forget the recent past and its unpleasantness. He was fluent in Spanish—or had been earlier when he had served as a Peace Corps volunteer in Bolivia. He had thought about returning to Bolivia for this getaway, but decided he would like to see Peru and visit Machu Picchu. Somehow he had failed to visit that famous site during his three Peace Corps years in neighboring Bolivia.

This trip was expensive, and he had flown first class to Lima, a luxury to which he decided he was entitled. And he could afford luxury for this trip. He had skimmed enough money from client accounts to cover the cost of a bit of post-divorce high living. That he had taken money from his clients' accounts did not disturb him. *I'm good at investing, and I make money for my clients,* he rationalized. *They come out ahead when they trust me, and they should be willing to pay more than the paltry standard commissions for my expertise.*

The finance and investment worlds in which Ted worked had increasingly become international. The days of neighborhood banks were long passed. Ted had made the effort to become well versed with international investment opportunities, and he offered them to his clients. With his knowledge of Spanish and South American cultures, he felt he could recognize Latin American opportunities for the enrichment of his clients. He subscribed to the *Miami Herald*, believing it to be the best American newsprint source of Latin American financial news. He clipped and copied articles that supported his actions, and forwarded them to his clients along with personal notes.

Some international investments allowed Americans to hide assets from the Internal Revenue Service. Although Ted scrupulously avoided directly suggesting such tax avoidance financial arrangements to his clients, he did manage to suggest in subtle but unmistakable ways means of sheltering money in investments of these types to his more affluent clients. Rules were not to be broken, but bending them a bit fit within his code of ethics. "Everybody does it." And his Spanish fluency helped him find rule-avoidance opportunities Latin America.

Ted had connected with a cocaine dealer in New York, and he expected to be rewarded handsomely for smuggling some of that product back to the States on this trip. He was confident he could obtain some that had not been cut or diluted with talcum powder or other inert ingredients. He would hold out some for his personal use, but he would sell most of it. Even without trying to bargain for the best price—he was concerned that doing that might lead to unpleasant consequences—his profit would be generous.

His personal use of cocaine was modest, or so he felt. In fact, he usually managed to limit his drug use to weekends. Saturdays were often lonely times in his post-divorce life. Cocaine helped with that. He had an established relationship with one supplier for whom he would smuggle some of the product through customs on his return from Peru. The money thus earned would help to support this trip and his choice of high-end accommodations. He would return to penury later, when he returned to the real world, when he had squandered the cocaine-smuggling pay-off.

His plan was to take a laptop computer with all of its innards removed. Plastic bags of powdered cocaine would fill their space during his return trip. He supposed travelers from the Andean region would be suspected of carrying drugs and be selected for baggage search in some random way. But he was confident that he would appear to be an honest businessman. He would travel dressed in a dark blue suit and conservative necktie, the typical attire of a traveling Latin-American business man. He would be expected to be carrying a laptop computer. Surely every modern business traveler did. Perhaps, maybe, he thought, he could use his Spanish fluency and familiarity with Bolivia to make future trips to South America for the drug dealer who would pay him for the drugs he smuggled home on this jaunt.

This modest effort at smuggling cocaine was to be, in Ted's mind, the opening move in a much larger gambit. Assuming—and assumptions when dealing with the margins of the law were always tenuous—that all went well, and especially assuming that the Peruvian drug dealer would impress him as trustworthy, Ted could, indeed would, build profitably upon this initial venture and the contacts involved. He knew he would need a reliable source if he were to enter the cocaine traffic world, and he was sufficiently cautious and experienced to believe that the South American drug business would have many potential pitfalls. His Spanish proficiency would help. Ultimately, however, he would succeed or fail depending on whom he partnered with in Peru. He needed a partner who would be both reliable and discreet. He hoped he might find leads to such a person on this trip. But maybe not. This trip was to be a vacation. This trip was intended as a break from his failed-marriage past. But one never knows. One must be ready to seize opportunities if and when they appeared.

Stretched out on his hotel bed, Ted paged through the *Fodor's Travel Guide* that he had picked up from a stall in the Miami airport and reviewed tourist options in Lima. *Okay,*he thought, *I have today here in Lima before flying to Cuzco tomorrow. I think I should go to the Museo Larco Herrera to see its pottery and then go to the Museo de Oro, the gold museum.* The ancient pottery at the Museo Larco was described by *Fodor's* as exceptional. On the other hand, many of the pieces at the gold museum are modern fakes, *Fodor's* told him, and not the historic artifacts they were advertised as. But interesting and gold and worth seeing, nonetheless. *I'll get lunch at one of the museums, and then come back here for dinner and a better night's sleep than I had on the flight here.*

It was midmorning when the taxi dropped him at the Museo Larco. The taxi driver assured him that there was a café at the museum where he could get lunch. Ted promised a generous tip if the taxi would pick him up again at one o'clock. He would get lunch at noon, an early hour for midday meals in Peru, he knew. The café would be open but mostly empty at that time.

The pottery and textiles exhibited at the museum were indeed exceptional, he felt. The Chimú pottery impressed him. The facial features of figures were realistic, probably representing real people, he supposed. Some of them appeared to be representing diseased human beings. *Could a modern physician make diagnoses based on these figures?* he wondered. Wandering about, he found a large room separated from the main exhibit area. It contained shelf after shelf of impressive pottery figures. Perhaps he should have allowed more time. He lunched in the museum's café, avoiding the attractive salad bar. He had learned during his Peace Corps years not to trust Latin American salads, however attractive they might appear. He ordered a Coca-Cola, specifying that it be brought to him in the bottle with a glass that contained no ice. On schedule, he met his taxi as arranged.

In the afternoon the gold museum surprised him. Whereas all of the items at the Museo Larco were carefully displayed and arranged so as to relate them to their sites and times of origins, those at the Museo de Oro were not always carefully presented. And there were so many smaller items casually set out that they lost their glamor. *Better lighting would help,* he mused. There were also scores and scores of weapons of various types from not only Peru but many locations in the world. "This stuff is just whatever the founder collected," Ted said to himself, softly but aloud. Gold objects should not appear ordinary, he felt. Here, somehow they did. Putting them on display together with the collection of weapons reduced their stature. Moreover, security seemed lax. Most of the time, he and the few other visitors were not visible to one of the few guards.

Impulsively, and not knowing quite why he did it, Ted picked up a gold figure from a counter and dropped it into his jacket pocket. Perhaps two and one-half inches tall, it was a man with a crooked back. *A remote cousin of Kokopelli,* he mused. He had seen Kokopelli figurines at the Heard Museum in Phoenix. Worth something, he wondered, and how much? He could easily get it back to the States undetected in a pocket, he felt. Then how could he sell it? Perhaps his cocaine dealer would know. Maybe he could donate it to a museum and get a tax deduction. But a museum would want to know how he got it. He would find a way to sell it. Perhaps one of his investment clients would be interested in a gold artifact from Peru.

Back at the Wyndham Airport Hotel, Ted found a table in the ground floor restaurant/bar. He ordered a martini, dry, on the rocks, with two olives. Plymouth gin, which the waiter assured him the bar stocked. A knock-off from Argentina, he assumed.

He should switch to pisco sours, he thought, but not tonight. Not yet. He liked martinis; pisco was okay, but not the equal of good gin. He had finished one drink and ordered a second when his Peruvian contact arrived. "Eduardo," he greeted Ted. "*¿Como Está? ¿Como le va?*"

"*Bien, gracias. ¿Y Usted?*"

"I am well, thank you," his Peruvian friend replied, switching to English and dropping his voice. "We must speak softly here, and in English." They continued chatting and enjoying martinis while making plans for the return to Ted of his altered, cocaine-transporting laptop computer. They would meet and make the transfer at the time of his return flight in the usually crowded and noisy second level of the terminal building, directly connected by a bridge to the hotel. That they would be surrounded by travelers eating and buying last minute gifts would afford them anonymity for the exchange.

"There is a problem, however." Ted did not want to hear this. Problems, problems, real or imagined, always meant more costs. "My friend, our contact person with the *cocaineros*, our supplier, wants more money. I tell him 'no,' but he insists."

"I see," Ted replied. "But I have problems as well. My dealers in New York think the cocaine is being cut. Perhaps with talcum powder. We can't have that. Before we can have any discussion of price, we need to be absolutely certain of the quality of the drug." In fact, Ted had no reason to doubt the purity of the cocaine he was receiving, but he wanted to take the initiative, to be the aggressor, in this conversation.

"Oh, no. This is good stuff. It is very pure that I supply to you. I am getting it from Ollantaytambo in the Urubamba Valley. There is nothing better anywhere."

"Okay. Let's leave it as it is. You are providing me with good drug; I am paying a fair price."

Following the departure of his Peruvian friend, Ted ordered a very North American dinner of steak and French fried potatoes. Then early to bed. Tired, he slept well.

. . .

CHARLES MARTIN was a native of Mansfield, Ohio. Tall and trim with sandy brown hair, he was the eldest of three children. He had aspired to be an athlete, running the half mile on his high school track team and a second stringer on the school's basketball team. He was a good student, with a 3.8 grade point average. Well liked by his classmates, they chose him as class president in his senior year. His father worked at an auto repair shop and was admired by his fellow workers for his ability to assess mechanical problems quickly and accurately.

Charles enrolled at Baldwin Wallace College in Berea, Ohio. He tried out for both the varsity basketball and track teams, but failed to make the cut for either. He ran recreationally several miles each week, thus keeping himself physically fit. He majored in classics, one of only three in his class. Uncertain about career options, he surprised himself by enjoying both Greek and Latin. Perhaps he had an aptitude for languages, he thought to himself. During the summer after his freshman year, he found a job at nearby Cuyahoga Valley National Park. He worked at the Boston Store Visitors Center, explaining the construction and navigation of boats built in an earlier century at local shipyards and used on the Ohio and Erie Canal. Boston was a thriving community and canal shipping hub, until railroads entered the region in the late eighteen hundreds. Subsequently Charles found summer jobs at Shenandoah National Park. He viewed his duties there as principally helping tourists who embarked on trails too difficult for their level of fitness. It's easy taking a trail down from a ridge-top highway parking area; it's harder trekking back up.

During his senior year he found a site on the Internet extolling the virtues of the Peace Corps. Not yet ready to enter the job market and not knowing why or what employment he might seek as a classics major, the idea of a Peace Corps assignment appealed to him. Two phone calls and a series of email exchanges later resulted in a voucher for travel to Costa Rica. There he joined a group of similar neophytes immersed in Spanish language training and expecting a Peace Corps assignment in Latin America. He enjoyed the training—not only the language but also the cross-cultural preparation for a Latin American tour.

In Costa Rica he became friendly with Ted Hewes, another PCV—in-house slang for Peace Corps Volunteer, he learned. The two young men were compatible, and they enjoyed practicing their gestating Spanish with one another. When free of an evening, they sometimes found their way to a local bar for a *cerveza* or two, often joined by other newly minted PCVs.

Charles and Ted were each pleased when they both drew assignments to a group heading for the Altiplano, the high inter-mountain plateau of Bolivia. They would be working at separate but nearby locations to introduce hybrid potatoes to local farmers. These potatoes had been developed at a Bolivian national agricultural station. They were well adapted to growth in the harsh soil and weather conditions of the Bolivian inter-mountain plateau. Seed eyes for these potatoes were available at no cost to Bolivian farmers. As PCVs on the Altiplano, they were charged with promoting the use of these hybrids. Neither of the two young men had farming backgrounds, but they were both confident that they could meet the challenges that their Peace Corps assignments presented to them.

Growing potatoes was a major agricultural activity of the small farms—*fincas*—of the Altiplano. Charles and Ted were to offer to plant part of a farmer's fields with the hybrid seed pieces.

The farmer would then discover that the potatoes they had planted were larger than those from his personal seed piece stock.

"*¿De donde vienen estas semillas, estas plantas, estas papas?*" Where do these potatoes come from?

"They come from Bolivia. From your national agricultural program. They are available to you at no cost."

Both of the young PCVs became involved in the rural communities where they were stationed. Saturdays were market days. Residents from rural regions surrounding market towns brought goods they hoped to sell in the town's central plaza. They also purchased supplies to carry home in the llama wool *bolsas*—sacks—they brought with them to the market. Charles and Ted enjoyed these rural markets. Saturday markets also provided opportunities for the two PCVs to interact with local residents and further their community development efforts. Although many of the Aymara-speaking Altiplano adults had only limited Spanish, young schoolchildren were eager to display their school-acquired fluency and translate for their parents. That they passed on community development ideas to their parents gave the youngsters feelings of importance.

Sometimes on weekends the two men would take a local bus into La Paz, Bolivia's functional, but not official, capital. There they would find a room at the centrally located Hotel Sucre and explore the local handicraft markets of Calle Sagarnaga. That narrow street wound its way tortuously uphill behind the cathedral. It was the principal market place for indigenous handcrafts. And they would find dinner at one of the more upscale hotels or perhaps the rooftop Las Vegas restaurant. A treat and welcome escape from their own cooking of local produce from Altiplano town markets.

On some Saturday evenings they found entertainment in La Paz at a *peña* on Calle Sagarnaga. Seated on small chairs that might have been stolen from a kindergarten classroom, they sipped Chilean red wine and enjoyed joining in the singing of *cuecas*, folks songs to which Bolivians danced a stylized dance representing the courtship display of a rooster. Stand-up comics provided laughs to *Paceños*, the local attendees. Although the two Americans were reasonably fluent, the locally-oriented and politically-satirical humor often eluded them.

Charles finished his Peace Corps tour and returned to Ohio. He found a position on the faculty of a private high school teaching social studies. He enjoyed that work, and soon became a popular teacher. He coached soccer. *Futbol*, in Bolivian Spanish, he told his student athletes. Toss a ball to a Bolivian boy, he noted, and he will knock it down not touching it with his hands and trap it with his feet. *Manos*—hands on the ball—meant a foul.

He also precepted an after-school Spanish club, helping out the regular Spanish teacher, whose home life included three children and an overwhelmed wife. He made jokes about Spanish language idioms, calling them "idiots." Also, he explained that the two Spanish words for English 'to be,' *ser* and *estar*, were confusing and seemingly ridiculous not only to them but also to most rural South Americans, at least to the Bolivians he had worked among. "*¿Como está?*—how are you?" might be waggishly answered, "*Aquí estoy.*—I am here." This local joke was a play on the Spanish verb *estar*, to be. The Spanish word *como* might mean either "where" or "how." Thus the phrase might ask "where are you?" or "how are you?" That the question could be either in this sentence was funny because it had no parallel in Quechua or Aymara, the two regional indigenous languages.

Charles decided to return to Bolivia during the Christmas school holiday. There was something captivating about the Andean region. Maybe not so much captivating as capturing! Certainly it had captured him during his Peace Corps tour. He explored various options in the town library. Machu Picchu caught his attention. He had known of it during his Peace Corp stint, but had not visited it. A good Christmas break, he decided. A better idea than Bolivia. Although now creeping toward his forties, he was reasonably fit. He decided he would go to Peru and walk the trail from Cuzco to the Inca site.

He asked Delores, the increasingly important woman in his life, to accompany him. They did many outdoor things together, and he felt she would enjoy the Andes and the walk to Machu Picchu. However, Delores worked for an accounting firm and getting away at year's end was just not possible. Maybe a Caribbean cruise after April fifteen tax deadlines, she offered. He was not sure that a mega-sized cruise ship fit their style. Perhaps they could find a smaller and more adventure oriented voyage. He must research the expedition offerings of Lindblad. In any case, he would find more adventures that they could share. Adventure travel would appeal to both of them, he was sure, and bring them together, he hoped. Perhaps, hopefully, something that would expose her to environments and cultures like the rural Andean life that had so altered his thinking about the world.

Reflecting on his high-altitude Peace Corps days in Bolivia, he scheduled himself for seventy-two hours in Cuzco so that he could adjust to the altitude before beginning his hike. And he took Diamox during those three days. He anticipated that the exertion of the hike would increase the likelihood that he would experience *soroche*, the local name given to altitude sickness. His Peace Corps time in Bolivia had made him familiar with most of the health problems of high altitude, and he knew that he would need time to adapt to oxygen deprivation-engendered hyperventilation. That excess breathing would cause him to expel carbon dioxide and change the acid-base relationships in his body. His brain would not like that. Headache, sleeplessness, and abdominal upset would result. Diamox would offset the effects of hyperventilation, at least in part.

Shortly after arriving in Cuzco, Charles purchased some coca leaves from a vendor on the central plaza. He knew it to be a time-tested local remedy for *soroche*. He would chew those leaves while in Cuzco and also while walking the trail to Machu Picchu. In addition to the Diamox.

He had first met cocaine in Bolivia, and had continued as an occasional user upon returning to the States. In fact, he acknowledged to himself, he used cocaine pretty regularly. More often than he should, perhaps, probably. But only somewhat, he told himself. He carefully hid his usage, for he knew it would cost him his teaching job if it were discovered. Moreover, Delores would have strongly disapproved. He knew that cocaine was threatening this relationship, and that made him believe he should give it up. But somehow he could not. Addicted, he wondered?

His supplier visited him in his apartment quietly on weekday evenings. Here in Peru, he decided coca and its drug, cocaine, were acceptable and normal. Certainly readily available and widely used. At least he thought so. Perhaps he should supplement the leaves he would chew with some of the actual drug. And perhaps he should also acquire some to take back with him. That might bring him some money. The dealer who sold him the drug at home—an unsavory character at best, an opportunist, he was sure—would probably pay him for it, although only a fraction of its worth on the street. It would be easy to hide some cocaine from customs inspectors. Then, of course, he would have to hide it from Delores, and that might be more difficult.

Charles was fascinated by Cuzco. Cuzco was and is a city of red tile roofs. Cuzco is a city of tourists. Cuzco is a city of ceramic beads. Cuzco is a city of travel agents. Cuzco is a city of hostelries.

Cuzco is a modern city built upon the foundations of awesome Incan ruins. Cuzco is the gateway to Machu Picchu.

Cuzco caters to tourists. It offers first class hotels, good restaurants, and limitless opportunities to spend money. Charles enjoyed his three day stay there. The central plaza of Cuzco is surrounded by shops offering souvenirs and typical tourist items. *Artesanias* —locally hand-crafted items reflecting the indigenous culture—are readily available, especially the ceramic beads for which this area is famous and hand-woven textiles. So also prominently available are tee shirts and coffee mugs. He should buy a gift for Delores. Not now, but on the way back.

Many of Cuzco's hotels offer inhaled oxygen to their newly arrived guests. Oxygen provides rapid relief from *soroche*, but only for as long as the oxygen is being inhaled. Hotels also offer coca tea brewed from the leaves of coca plants to arriving guests as a remedy for *soroche*. A green tea containing only minimal amounts of the drug, it is, in fact, of little benefit for oxygen deprivation. Charles preferred to chew coca leaves as he had seen Bolivians do. Ultimately, he knew, he and other visitors must adapt to the altitude, and this takes about thirty-six hours. A retreat to a lower altitude is often in order for new arrivals, but Charles would need to adapt in the high altitude before beginning his trek to Machu Picchu.

Those travelers who arrive overland on the daily train from Puno on the shore of Lake Titicaca have already adapted to the Andean altitude and thus do not suffer when they reach Cuzco. Most of them are tourists coming from Bolivia; they experienced their adaptation illness in the high altitudes of that country. Also, those who take the long and tedious bus trip from coastal Arequipa, Peru, adapt during the long hours of their ride up from sea level.

Cuzco's status as the gateway to Machu Picchu contributes

to the retail activity of the city. Importantly for Charles, there
are shops offering supplies for persons who make the overland
hike to the Incan site. Many centrally located shops include out-
fitters providing gear for hikers who choose to approach Machu
Picchu via the mountainous trail. An inquiry at any of these
establishments will locate an experienced local guide. Charles
had researched the hike before leaving home, and felt he did not
need a guide. The ridge-top trail did not offer opportunities for
wandering off. And he had brought boots, a sleeping bag, and
hiking clothes with him. He did purchase some dried fruits and
jerky—dried beef in the United States, more likely dried goat
meat here, he realized. He did not know what if any cooking
options he would find on the Machu Picchu trail, so he wanted
to be prepared to survive on uncooked, dried food.

For those visitors who take the time to adapt to the altitude
Cuzco has much to offer. The cathedral built by early Spanish
conquistadores was constructed upon the foundations of an Inca
temple. While anxious to establish Christianity in Cuzco, the
early Spaniards recognized and capitalized upon the architec-
tural skills of the indigenous people. Working with no metals
stronger or less malleable than copper, the Incans cut massive
stone blocks and fit them together so closely that one cannot
insert a piece of paper between them. Today the stone masonry
of an Incan temple supports the cathedral walls erected by the
Spanish *conquistadores*.

Not far from Cuzco are the ruins at Pisac. Overlooking the
Vilcanota River, they constitute a major and important Inca for-
tified site. *Well worth visiting,* Charles thought ruefully. "Next
time," he said to himself. Also near Cuzco sit the massive ruins of
Sacsayhuaman. Constructed of huge stones, they appear to repre-
sent a fortification. But their site does not suggest what if anything
they were placed to defend. How this enormous structure could

have been erected by the early inhabitants remains a puzzling mystery. Charles had read about it. Perhaps—probably, certainly—worth a later visit, he thought. For the present, rest and altitude adaptation were first on his agenda.

For many arriving tourists—but not Charles—escape from *soroche* is provided by a prompt departure from Cuzco to the lower altitude of Machu Picchu. An early morning train after a headache-tormented, restless night brings one down through the valley of the Urubamba River to an altitude of about seven thousand feet, with Machu Picchu about one thousand feet above on a ridge. Modern tourist literature describes this river valley as "sacred." The only reason to apply this epithet to the region, Charles believed, was to promote tourist interest. No one knows what early inhabitants thought of this truly spectacular valley. Spaniards traveled it, but failed to find the lofty site of Machu Picchu. Before continuing on beyond the terminus for tourists, the river makes a horseshoe bend around towering Mount Huayna Picchu, the peak that the ridge housing the ruins of Machu Picchu abuts at its termination.

Expecting to meet other hikers on the trail to Machu Picchu, Charles was surprised to find himself alone for the entire trek. Most folks choose to spend Christmas with families, he supposed, not hiking a twenty-five mile trail in the Andes. But much trailside trash made it evident that these three days with no traffic were an anomaly. Late in the afternoon of his third hiking day, he arrived at the inn adjacent to the ruins. He was tired, sweaty, dirty, and hoping for a hot-water shower. Nevertheless, he felt good about himself and proud of the trek he had accomplished.

· · ·

TED caught a morning flight from Lima to Cuzco. He had booked into the Marriott El Convento Hotel, chosen from its Internet site and continuing the high-living style he had adopted for this trip. Knowing that he would experience *soroche*, he rested in his hotel room, ate lightly at lunch and dinner, and caught the first morning train down to Machu Picchu, escaping the effects of higher altitude as the train descended the Urubamba River Valley to the stop below the ridge-hugging ruins of the ancient Incan city.

CHAPTER TWO

Julia and Erica

LIFE WAS MEANT TO BE lived one day at a time. Julia Young believed that. What life might present tomorrow should be a problem for tomorrow, not today. Slender and inherently attractive, she eschewed cosmetics; she had read that the red dye in lipstick caused cancer in mice, at least when applied in enormous concentration. She wore her long, blond hair in a pony tail. She favored fringed skirts but not while working. Her boss was a very conservative man who wore a dark gray suit, white shirt, and solid color tie every day. Four-in-hand knot for the necktie; never a Windsor knot. For her part, Julia's work clothes always consisted of a dark skirt and white or light blue blouse. Often a scarf at the neck. Sometimes a brooch. A gold band on her left fourth finger. She was not married, but the ring avoided comments and suggestions she did not want to deal with.

Now into the second half of her thirties and trying to ignore and never to think about a fortieth birthday that loomed in a future she liked to believe was distant, she considered herself a free spirit. Free to do whatever her spirit moved her to do today. Except, of course, while working at a job that provided necessary income. And also except that her daughter, Erica, was about to turn eighteen. Some deeply recessed and in-bred maternal instincts imposed parenting responsibilities and limits on Julia's free spiritedness. Nonetheless, she hoped that she could set an example for her daughter of a life unconstrained by male-dominated, unjustifiably conventional, societal expectations. However, she acknowledged, one needed money and that meant holding a job.

She worked at a travel agency. She was facile with the Internet; her boss was not. She worked hard, often staying late. Her diligence earned her respect, and her employer increasingly relied upon her for much of the day-to-day operation of the agency. Recognizing her role and importance at the office, she asked for and received a pay raise. She enjoyed her employment position.

Julia had grown up in Manhattan as the only child of two hard-working parents. A nanny had taken her for walks and later bicycle rides in Central Park, provided that the weather was favorable. And provided that the nanny's boyfriend was not visiting.

Central park provided her with an outdoor environment, a place to relax and enjoy nature, albeit in the middle of the city. Sitting on a park bench one sunny afternoon, she watched a shirtless young man running on one of the paved trails. Okay, she thought to herself, if he can work on a suntan, so can I. She took of her blouse and bra, closing her eyes and enjoying the feeling of warmth that embraced her. Suddenly she became aware that someone had taken a seat beside her on the bench. Reaching for her clothes, she opened her eyes to discover that she now shared her sitting place with a middle-aged, fiftyish police officer. He smiled, nodded at her, and commented, "Yes, you should cover up. I would hate to have to arrest you for public nudity."

She attended a private school in New York. She was smart and did well, earning mostly A's. She aced the SATs. Rebelling against her parents' ideas of appropriate colleges and universities, she escaped up the Hudson River to SUNY in New Paltz. That she did not go to Radcliffe or Smith was the result of a rebellious spirit that her busy parents accepted as something she would grow out of. She earned spending money by posing nude at the university's art department classes. She became intrigued with tarot cards and used them to tell the fortunes of her friends, although none of her fellow students treated those foretelling cards with the respect that she accorded them. She decided on a math major, expecting that it would teach her about the odds of various card combinations.

Julia met Ted Hewes at a mixer given by his fraternity during rush week. She had no interest in the fraternity or in its party, but she yielded to the call of free beer. She never knew why she was attracted to Ted at that event. She was, however. Soon they were dating and not long after that sexually active partners. When summer brought the end of the school year, they separated, each promising to "stay in touch," each expecting to resume their relationship when classes resumed in the fall.

She found a summer job waiting tables at a Catskill Mountains resort. Not challenging employment, but hard work with long and tiring hours. It allowed her to earn money, and she found companionship among her coworkers.

Julia missed her menstrual period in June. She purchased a pregnancy test kit in a local drugstore. It confirmed her suspicion. She was pregnant. She considered seeking an abortion. But she was a woman, and maternity was a normal woman thing. She would bear this child and be its mother. She decided not to return to the university for the fall semester. She made no attempt to contact Ted. Her mother welcomed her upon her return to New

York City and was excited about her pregnancy. Her father grudg-
ingly accepted her and was furious about her pregnancy. "Date
rape," he said angrily. He suggested an abortion. "No, never,"
she responded. "And it wasn't rape at all. I wanted sex with him.
I seduced him." Her daughter, whom she named Erica, arrived
on Christmas Eve.

Julia needed an income. A college drop-out with no more
than summer job experience and no specialized skills had limited opportunities. She took a position as a cocktail waitress at an
upscale hotel lobby bar. The salary was modest, but a few sug-
gestive hip movements and friendly comments usually produced
generous tips. When a customer suggested an assignation, she
simply replied that her husband kept a tight rein on her, tossing
her head in a nod to the burly bartender. He was, in fact, protective of her and seemed to take pride in acting in a shepherding
marital role.

With some reluctantly but graciously accepted financial help
from her parents, she rented a two-bedroom apartment and hired
a nanny to provide daytime care for Erica. Guatemalan, the nanny
might teach Erica Spanish words, Julia hoped. Erica was not long
out of a crib, however, when Julia came home unannounced to
collect some papers she had forgotten when she had left in the
morning. She found the nanny and a Latino man engaged in
sexual intercourse on the living room couch while Erica sat on
the floor holding a favorite "stuffy." Julia promptly dispatched
both the sitter and her boyfriend. Julia's mother cared for Erica
for four days until a replacement sitter was found.

There was much about Erica's youth in New York that repli-
cated Julia's youth. She blossomed into a beautiful, fair-skinned
and blond, young woman in her teen years. Moreover, she
developed many of the liberation attitudes of her mother. On
several occasions during school vacations she joined in protest

demonstrations in Central Park. The issues were important, she supposed, but the greater significance of these events was that it brought many young people together to champion causes that politicians tended to ignore.

Erica was smart. She attended The Misses Masters' School in Dobbs Ferry, New York, with grandparent financial assistance. She was a good student, earning mostly A's. Popular with her peers, she was elected "head of house" in the dormitory where she lived. She was giving serious thought to college. It would have to be one that allowed a liberal thinker to feel at home and find like-minded friends. Oberlin in Ohio was currently at the top of her list. Radcliffe also, but that sister institution to Harvard seemed large, perhaps too large for her.

About two years after her return to New York and with Erica under the care of a nanny, Julia found a job at a travel agency and gave up being a cocktail waitress. The travel agency positioned Julia with an opportunity to earn money that her parents would not have approved of. She was now a self-confident, mature adult, however. She no longer needed more parental approval than was necessary to maintain the modest flow of cash that supplemented her salary. She could choose what to tell her parents and what not to tell them. Moreover, this opportunity potentially promised complete independence from her parents, even in costly New York City, even while supporting her daughter.

Julia was a modest marijuana and occasional cocaine user. One of her suppliers connected her to his source, a man who found her travel agency access to airline schedules and flight-booking data of use in scheduling the "mules" who carried his cocaine from its Andean origins. They should arrive in Miami or Houston at the airport's busiest arrival times, thus hoping for a cursory transit through immigration.

Julia did her best to keep her involvement secret, not because of moral or ethical concerns, but simply because she did not want to compromise the modest but important flow of cash it provided nor lose her job. Her employer would not have tolerated this activity. However, she knew what she was doing was wrong, deceitful, unethical. She should give it up, perhaps accept society's moral standards, perhaps be more thoughtful about role modeling for her daughter. But she needed the money.

Why Julia and Erica were in Peru and about to celebrate Christmas and Erica's eighteenth birthday at Machu Picchu was a question that had no meaning for Julia. They were in Peru because that is where they were when they left the cruise ship at Salaverry. The ship was there to permit passengers to visit the nearby ruins.

Julia's travel agency position had made the under-booked cruise affordable. She had booked the trip when she discovered that it was largely under-subscribed. She convinced the cruise company that it should provide gratuitous accommodations on one of its trips to her as an agent of a New York travel agency that frequently booked passengers on Caribbean cruises. Thus, she, the agent, might be encouraged to suggest the Pacific cruise to future clients. She did, however, have to pay for Erica's passage.

They had joined the cruise in San Diego. The ship docked at Salaverry to allow its passengers to visit the Chimu ruins at Chan Chan. Those eighteen-hundred-year-old structures were sculpted of clay and sand. Row after sculptured row, the ruins evoked patterns of waves. Along one wall the early artisans had created images of marine forms. Geometric frescoes had retained their original pigmentation. Although now protected by metal roofs erected on poles, the ruins had survived century after century without this protection because the area is one of the driest deserts in the world. It never rains. Almost never. In fact, minor damage from a modest rainstorm some years earlier had led to the construction of the corrugated metal roofs over them. Some of the impressive original pigmented decorations were still visible and awed Erica and Julia.

Acting on a whim, Julia and Erica decided to leave the cruise. They simply walked away from the cruise ship's land tour of the ruins. Their luggage was limited to backpacks; it was easily taken with them. Unnoticed by the crowd-shuttling tour guide, they made their way into Salaverry. There they found a modest ocean-front hotel. Looking out from the malecon across the beach, they were intrigued by the reed boats in use by local fishermen. Cut off at the stern, they seemed to be half boats.

The next morning they found a taxi. The driver offered to take them to the ruins. His brother was a guide there, and he could get them a good price for a guided tour. "No," Julia said in her fragmentary Spanish. "We have seen the ruins. We want to go to Trujillo. There will be buses from there to Lima, *¿No es cierto?*"

"*Claro.*" Of course. Bargaining followed, and Julia ultimately accepted a price that she thought was probably excessive. There were no other taxis in sight, however, so she felt that further haggling was not really an option.

Trujillo proved to be an old city that enchanted Julia and Erica. Built around a plaza with municipal buildings on one side, it had a hotel fronting on the plaza. The architecture of the buildings and some statuary on the plaza emphasized the colonial antecedents of the city. In fact, they would learn, Trujillo was the city where Bolivar organized his army that liberated Peru and Bolivia from the Spaniards. Bolivar, she was told by a placard in the town's central square, was a Venezuelan who led much of the effort to expel Spain from northern South America. The people of Bolivia, originally Alto Peru (Upper Peru) took his name for their nation when they broke away from Peru.

Julia and Erica checked into the Hotel Tourista on the town plaza. It appeared to be the town's only hotel, certainly the only one evident to them. They were shown a room on the top floor. The clerk told them it would be cooler during the day and warm in the evening because of its fourth-floor location. As they toted their luggage up the stairs, the women wondered if there were other guests—indeed, if there had been any other guests in recent weeks. As they entered the room a solitary cockroach scampered under a baseboard. The room seemed clean otherwise, however. The double bed had linen that appeared to be clean and fresh. They would have to struggle with sagging springs that would roll them together during the night, however. Returning to the lobby and enquiring of the clerk, they found a small restaurant where they ate dinner.

A bus took them from Trujillo to Lima. The bus was modern, and its seats were comfortable. Not like any North American bus Julia had experienced. In Lima they found an inexpensive hostel. Deciding to spend a day in Lima, they walked in the old, colonial era city center, and enjoyed looking at the facades of the old buildings.

The old section of Lima between the city's two principal plazas fascinated them. They were awed by the many elegantly worked wooden balustrades gracing the fronts of buildings and reaching into sequestered courtyards. The ornate dark woodwork impressed them greatly. Upscale residences in old colonial structures, they supposed. And upscale shops at the ground level. They passed a Sears store. It appeared to be a high-end, fashionable, upscale emporium, not the mass-market vendor it was in the U.S.

They visited the Museo de la Inquisicion y del Congreso. The walk to the inquisition museum took them through a neighborhood that was unenticing. It seemed uninviting and somehow threatening. The inquisition museum, however, was fascinating. They found its architecture and interior woodwork awesome. Sitting in the ornate, elaborate judicial chamber, they could imagine sentences of torture and death being imposed on unfortunate people accused of heresy and standing trial before an unsympathetic ecclesiastical court.

Despite its interesting historical and colonial aspects, Lima was a big city, as traffic-bogged as New York. They could see and tolerate that at home!

Before dinner, Julia and Erica sat at a sidewalk café and enjoyed ceviche with pisco. Lima fascinated them, they acknowledged, but it was not what they wanted for a vacation. They would enjoy dinner and then return to the hostel, ready to depart the next day on a morning flight.

They flew on LAN, the Chilean airline that served much of South America, to Cuzco, heading for Machu Picchu. Julia had booked clients there, and knew it to be spectacular. A "World Heritage Site," in fact. Their checked backpacks, however, did not make the flight from Lima. They sought out a LAN agent, who apologized while telling them that this happened sometimes. Maybe their bags went to Iquitos; a flight headed there had left Lima at about the same time. Check back later tonight or tomorrow, he advised. Neither "later tonight" nor "tomorrow" produced their packs. They did, however, enjoy Cuzco. Erica was enchanted by the many and varied beads sold by curbside vendors there. One could market them profitably in New York, she commented to her mother. The Incan stone work that had been incorporated into the walls of the cathedral greatly impressed them.

Despite their lack of luggage, Julia and Erica decided to continue their planned trip to Machu Picchu with simply the clothes they were wearing plus changes of underwear and a few toiletries that they purchased at a shop in Cuzco. They booked train tickets and rode down the Urubamba River Valley, awed by the spectacular scenery. The train hugged the side of the steep valley, while the river tumbled beside it. Descending from the train, they found that they would take a jitney bus up to the ridge-top ruins and the adjacent hotel. One other couple left the train, albeit from another car; they would join them on the bus.

"I'm Julia, and this is Erica, my daughter," Julia introduced herself.

"Hi. I'm Harriet, and this is Mark, my husband. I guess you're going up to the ruins too."

"Yes, we hope to stay at the inn there."

"And we're booked there. I guess we'll be spending Christmas together."

"I suppose there won't be many other guests there at Christmas, so we may see a good bit of each other. Where are you from?"

"New York. And you?"

"Ditto. New York."

"How about that! Well, it's a big city."

CHAPTER THREE

Mark and Harriet

MARK AND HARRIET MET while they were students at Taft, a New England college-preparatory school in Connecticut. Their families each managed to afford the steep tuition for a school that provided both excellent education and a well lubricated track to admission to Yale. They were both good students. Mark Strong was an athlete and played varsity lacrosse. Harriet Manning found herself excited by participating in the school's drama club's production of Eugene O'Neill's *Long Day's Journey Into Night*. She played the drug-addicted mother. Thinking back, Harriet believed that the close friendship between them may have been incubating during those prep school years.

Along with nearly one-third of their graduating Taft classmates, they both gained admission to Yale. There Harriet chose a major in art history. With its own museum and substantial collections, Yale had great strength in academic programs focused on art. Mark opted for studies of engineering, choosing a major in mechanical engineering. Originally a separate institution, Yale's Sheffield School of Engineering offered strong programs in various aspects of engineering. He believed his engineering studies would be important as he launched a career in the business world. Entering the arena of finances, he found the material he had studied at Yale only indirectly relevant, but he recognized that the discipline of his studies taught him to approach problems of the business world with success-engendering rigor.

Their relationship blossomed at Yale, although they lived in separate residential colleges, she in Silliman, he in Branford. In the fall they rode resurrected ancient street cars to Yale Bowl for football games. There were parties following the games at various campus venues, often lasting late into Saturday night, usually offering gin in grapefruit juice. Sea breezes, these drinks were called, for a reason that was obscure at best. The couple dated with increasing frequency, and soon found themselves in her single-room bed on many Saturday nights.

Some Saturday nights were less alcoholic and more civil, if no less enjoyable. The Schubert Theater located across a street corner from Yale's Old Campus, was a frequent venue for New York-bound stage shows. Tickets were not expensive. Mark and Harriet often took advantage of these pre-Broadway stagings.

On Saturday nights when there were no football or other sports-related evening events, they often went to Mory's. With friends, they sometimes ordered a "green cup," a popular green drink of mysterious composition served in an oversized, two-handled drinking vessel and meant to be passed around a table. On some Saturdays the Whiffenpoofs would assemble at "the tables down at Mory's…and the magic of their singing [would] cast its spell." On other nights they were entertained at Mory's by The Spizzwinks or the Sons of Orpheus and Bacchus. (O&Bs). Small a capella singing groups were a fixture of the Yale scene dating back well before the Eli days of Cole Porter.

Mark and Harriet were both from Ohio. "Buckeyes," they called themselves as did many Ohioans, referring to the tree common in Ohio that had been adopted by Ohio State University as a nickname for its athletic teams. Mark's family lived in Dayton. Harriet grew up in Chagrin Falls, an exurb east of Cleveland.

Harriet's parents mounted a coming-out party for Harriet during her Yale freshman year Christmas vacation. She vigorously resisted the idea initially, but relented when her father told her it would be of major importance to his construction company's business. He and his family needed to be well known in the greater Cleveland community, and to appear prosperous, even if that was only marginally true. However, she made it a condition of her acceptance that she be allowed to invite Mark and that he be her escort at the ball. Despite her early misgivings, the party and the weekend activities surrounding it that engulfed her and Mark turned out to be exciting and fun.

With generous introductions by a major construction client, Harriet's father was able to book the Gates Mills Hunt Club for the event. The Hunt Club—which still held anachronistic fox hunts—was the premier venue for high society events in the Cleveland area. That the party could take place there told all of her father's business colleagues that he was successful. It would mean new business for him.

Harriet and Mark were married in June following their Yale commencement. Commencement, Harriet mused, was an odd designation for the ceremonies marking the end of four college years. She understood, however, that the occasion bore that name to indicate that graduating students would follow their Yale years with new entries into their upcoming careers. For Mark and Harriet those new entries were jobs in the financial world centered in New York City's Wall Street offices. Harriet found a position as an analyst at Goldman Sachs. She was not quite sure what she would analyze, but she was confident that she would succeed at it. Mark found a similar position at Lehman Brothers Holdings.

They were both computer-literate—highly skilled, in fact—and expert in and at home with the logic of computer systems and languages.

How did Yale prepare them for these careers, Harriet asked Mark at dinner one night. They talked about their college studies and together realized that what they had learned at Yale was to think critically and analytically. That was much more important than the individual disciplines they studied.

Good jobs for both of them. Good opportunities in New York's global-reaching center of finance. Not, however, until after a honeymoon in Bermuda. They loafed on the island's small and frequently private beaches. They rode bicycles on the motorless avenues and roadways. They ate in good restaurants. They walked about the town holding hands.

The newlyweds established themselves in an apartment on New York City's Upper West Side, not far from the Museum of Natural History. They enjoyed visits to that museum, Harriet especially attracted to the excellent examples of indigenous artwork. Mark most enjoyed the dinosaurs. Their relationship to birds was nicely explained, but it seemed extraordinary to him.

Their careers were taking off—or should have been. In fact, hers was; she enjoyed her work and won an early promotion. Mark's career, indeed his life, floundered. He was unhappy with the person who supervised his work. Moreover, he began using marijuana, and with increasing frequency, cocaine, introduced to it by a coworker. He managed to hide his growing addiction from Harriet, using the drug during the day and relying on a steadily increasing number of martinis to carry him through dinnertimes and evenings. His drinking worried Harriet. She began thinking about a vacation trip that might create a change in venue and relief from the job-related stress that she felt promoted his drinking. That idea was set aside, however, when Mark was fired from his job. He had been caught by his supervisor while in a stairwell rolling a joint.

Without recommendations, Mark found it difficult to gain new employment. He found a job driving a taxi. It kept him busy, but provided only minimal remuneration. He frequently stopped for a drink or two at a bar before returning to their apartment. To Harriet's dismay, he showed up one evening with a tattoo on his lower left arm. Somehow, this event released the long-suppressed anger and discouragement that she felt regarding her husband's behavior. She vented her anger noisily and banished him from their bed to the living room couch. His response was to return to the tattoo parlor the next day for further adornment.

Harriet struggled with her increasingly difficult and frustrating marital situation. She loved Mark—at least the Mark she had married. She was sure that his present degradation was the result of losing his job. She was aware of his cocaine use but not the extent of it or the events that caused his job dismissal. It was November, and her family would expect them at Christmas time. Somehow she had to avoid that encounter. Walking from the subway to her office building, she passed a travel agency. Impulsively, she entered, and she booked a trip that would take her and Mark to Machu Picchu for the Christmas holidays. Away from jobs, away from family, away from New York. She had to find a better life for them, and going to a faraway place seemed to her a way to start looking for that life.

Off the train from Cuzco to Machu Picchu and having encountered Julia and Erica, Harriet queried their two fellow arrivals, "You're looking for the bus up?"

"Yeah, we are."

"So are we."

The two couples—Mark and Harriet and Julia and Erica—chatted, expanding on their brief self-introductions. They found and climbed into the small bus that would take them up to the inn. Just before the bus rolled out onto the road, Ted joined them. He had been on the train with them, but not in a car with either of the couples. He thought he recognized Julia, was certain that he did, in fact, but decided to say nothing—at least not yet. The bus was soon under way, climbing up the serpentine road to the ruins and the adjoining inn. The newly acquainted tourists chatted, the two couples having discovered that they were both from New York City.

About halfway up the tortuous road, the bus stopped. The driver got out.

"Oh, hell!" Mark grumbled. "A third world, nonfunctioning bus, I guess."

Presently the driver returned. In his hand he held three orchids. Bowing gracefully, he presented the wild-growing blossoms to Harriet, Erica, and Julia.

"Hey," Erica exclaimed. "I like this." She turned to the driver and thanked him. The others also spoke up, offering their thanks.

Entering the inn, the arriving guests were greeted at the check-in counter by Fernando. He accepted their passports, wrote their names and passport numbers in a log book, and gave them two separate registration cards to complete. "Why two registration cards?" Mark asked.

"One will be collected in the morning by an agent from the Ministry of Tourism. Except, of course, tomorrow is Christmas. But he'll probably be by later to pick it up. Perhaps after New Year's Day."

"And what does the ministry do with the card? Are we suspects or something?"

"Oh, no, not suspects. The ministry does this for all guests in all hotels in Peru. And they'll file the cards."

"From all the hotels in Peru. It must be big file."

"I guess so. But I don't ask. I just do my job!"

Fernando handed the arriving guests their room keys. "The rooms are on the second floor. This is a holiday, so we have no porters today. In fact, Humberto, the cook, and I are the only ones here today and tomorrow. If you would place your bags at the foot of the stairs, I'll carry them up in a bit."

"Oh, no. We can handle them."

"Good. Then come back down for a drink at the bar. This is Christmas Eve, and all bar drinks will be free."

As the newly registered guests were turning to the stairs, Charles walked in the front door. Sweaty, tired, and dirty, he looked forward to a shower, a good dinner, and a clean bed. Turning at the sound of the door opening, Ted saw and recognized him. "Charles Martin, what in God's name are you doing here?"

"Holy shit, Ted! What are *you* doing here?" He shrugged his pack off his shoulders and set it on the floor.

Ted walked to greet Charles. "Hey, I'd give you a hug, but you don't look very huggable at the moment. How long has it been?"

"A good many years, I guess. I'm a school teacher now, off on holiday break. I walked here from Cuzco. Let me get checked in and cleaned up. Then we'll catch up. I want to know what you are doing."

"Right. Fernando here will check you in. And drinks are on the house tonight, he says."

"Good. I need a drink. A tall, cold beer, perhaps. *Paceña*. No, that's Bolivian, unless things have changed. Whatever, just so long as it's cold and wet."

Charles completed his registration card. "We have one more guest arriving today," Fernando commented. "The inn will be mostly empty. Dinner will be at six-thirty."

"I look forward to it. Last night was dried jerky and a bottle of Inka Cola on the trail."

CHAPTER FOUR

Marta and Olaf

THEIR LUGGAGE HASTILY STOWED in their rooms, the new arrivals made their way to the inn's lounge. The open bar would be welcome after a long day of travel. There they met Olaf and Marta Bergstrom and Richard and Rosa. They had arrived the previous day, become acquainted with one another, and already spent many hours visiting the ruins. With introductions made, Ted commented, "We've become a bit acquainted on the ride up from the train. Where are you folks from?" He turned to the Nordic couple. "Olaf doesn't sound like a Peruvian name. I guess Marta could be."

"Well," Olaf responded, "we're Swedish. We're stationed at the Swedish embassy in Lima. With things being quiet for the holiday, we thought we would spend Christmas here." Although Olaf and Marta Bergstrom presented themselves as Swedish and implied that they were diplomats at the Swedish embassy in Lima, they were, in fact, Russian spies, albeit low-level ones. They were employed at the Swedish embassy, he as a driver and she as a housekeeper. Those apparently menial positions allowed them to overhear conversations and sometimes recover documents before they disappeared into a shredder. Whether any of the conversations they overheard or documents they obtained from the Swedish embassy in Peru were of interest to Moscow was a question they simply did not ask. They passed on what they could without judging its importance.

In reality, Olaf was Swedish. He was tall, blond, and rugged. He enjoyed outdoor activities, and was an excellent skier. In good weather he took long hikes on wooded mountain trails. Women were attracted to Olaf, and he had enjoyed a number of brief romances before meeting Marta. Once coupled with Marta, he was faithful and devoted to her.

Marta was not Swedish. She was Russian, although she had lived in Stockholm with Olaf for most of her adult life. She had a typical broad Slavic face. Like her husband, she was also blond. Her hair was cut to fall well above her shoulders. They had met at a youth hostel in Finland when both were university students. She enjoyed outdoor activities with Olaf, although she eschewed some of the more strenuous outings that he undertook. She also had a domestic streak in her personality. She enjoyed cooking. And she took up needle point, stitching Norse designs on occasions when Olaf was away on one of his outings.

A weekend romance while university students led to more encounters at various European venues. Their academic schedules allowed them time to meet and travel together frequently, and as they did so their relationship blossomed and took on permanence. They hiked the Swiss Alps together; they splurged on a trip to the Canary Islands. It was there that Olaf proposed to Marta—on a night after they visited a nude beach where Marta cast off her clothes and teased him into doing the same. On the volcanic island, Lanzarote, they felt the warm ground and rode camels.

They were married in Sweden shortly after Olaf received his degree from Darlana University. They settled in Stockholm.

Olaf found a job in a travel agency; Marta worked in a bank. In Sweden, as in much or Europe, fluency in English was expected, and it was, in fact, a necessity for Olaf's employment. Marta's English was not quite as proficient as that of her husband, but she was improving rapidly.

Marta found that Russian friends working at the Soviet embassy in Stockholm were interested in what she could tell them about recent currency transactions. They paid her for information that she gathered from conversations she overheard at the bank where she worked. Sometimes she passed on papers she recovered from wastebaskets. That this evident trash should be of interest to Russia seemed curious to her, but she did not worry about it. She was grateful for the money. She felt like a spy! It was exciting!

One day a client at the travel agency where Olaf worked asked for information about Peru. Olaf knew nothing about Peru, but did know how to find information on the Internet. He asked the client to return the next day when he would have material for him. As Olaf researched Peru and South America, he became increasingly intrigued with opportunities there

Olaf talked with Marta at dinner that night. His brain was incubating an idea that perhaps they might like Peru and that perhaps they might have skills and background that they could exploit there. Intrigued, Marta invited two of her Russian diplomat friends to their apartment for dinner that Saturday. Over kir before dinner, they talked about what they might do for Russia in Peru.

Russia, it seemed, might be interested in learning about and perhaps infiltrating the cocaine trade. It was not the drug that attracted their attention. It was the backdoor route from Peru to North America that interested them. The Andes were a major source of lithium for the United States. That metal was vital to all light-weight electronics, and might be of great strategic importance in any international conflict. They would be well paid if they could position themselves so as to have access to diplomatic interchanges in Peru. That most of what they did learn and passed on seemed to be trivial and of little consequence was not of concern to them. They were happy for the Peruvian *soles* they received.

The Bergstroms were cocaine users. They had no moral concerns about the drug. The extra money they earned at what they considered harmless information gathering in the embassy helped them afford their recreational cocaine purchases. That the drug might be addicting did not threaten them. They were sufficiently mature to avoid that threat, they assumed. However, they knew that their Swedish employers would not tolerate their drug use. Moderation and secrecy were necessary.

They had found that packages apparently casually addressed and tossed into the diplomatic pouch arrived safely at the addresses of their Stockholm partners. The designation "diplomatic pouch" suggested secrecy. They knew, however, that it was just an ordinary mailbag that was not subject to customs on arrival. Using this avenue, the Bergstroms had become regular suppliers to narcotic distributors in Sweden. They were handsomely paid for this activity; the money thus earned was deposited in a bank account in Stockholm. Their retirement fund, they believed.

Soon-to-arrive Arthur, another guest, might be a threat, they would shortly discover. Were he to learn of their cocaine use and their shipment of it in the Swedish diplomatic pouch, their embassy positions might be at risk. They might even face deportation or, much worse, arrest by Peruvian authorities. They were not employed at positions where any sort of diplomatic immunity might protect them.

The guests began assembling in the inn's lounge. Located to

the left off the entrance hall as one entered the inn and across the hall from the dining room, the lounge was an obvious gathering place for inn guests. Fernando, the inn manager, had furnished it with comfortable chairs. He had installed a well-stocked bar along the wall across from the windows. He had decorated the room with large photographs of the ruins and with Andean textiles. The room was inviting and comfortable. Its ambiance invited conversation among newly arrived visitors.

Ted stepped up to the bar assuming the role of bartender. He offered to make drinks for all. "Pisco sours, everyone?" he asked. "Looks like there is plenty of pisco. It seems to be Peruvian," he commented as he examined the bottle's label. "Better that than the Bolivian pisco Charles and I had when we were there with the Peace Corps. Or Scotch? There's a bottle here. Johnny Walker. A knock-off from Argentina, I would guess, unless things have changed in the past decade. "

Erica spoke up, "We should include Fernando. I'll go get him." She left to look for their host.

"When you find him, see if you can get some lemons for the pisco sours."

"Right. I'll see what I can get." She headed for the kitchen.

Ted stepped away from the bar and took Julia by the arm. He steered her towards the window and away from the others. "Julia. You look lovely. I never would have dreamed that I might encounter you here."

"Nor I you, Ted. This is truly quite a surprise. Thank you. And you look well. I trust you are."

"I am. Just off a divorce. But meeting you here… Of course, I haven't stayed in touch or seen you lately, but somehow vacationing here at Machu Picchu doesn't seem like what you would do."

"Well, it just sort of happened. And maybe that's more like me than if I had carefully planned it. And I certainly didn't expect to find you here. In fact, I might have avoided this place if I knew you would be here."

"Is that beautiful young woman who I think she might be?" he asked.

"Yes, Ted, she's your daughter. But don't tell her. Just leave it. I've told her she is the product of a loving relationship that didn't last. But no more. Please. Keep it that way."

CHAPTER FIVE

Richard and Rosa

S HE CALLED HIM RICARDO, he called her Rosalita. Thrown together as graduate students, they soon were lovers. Their studies had brought them together, each from a different ethnic background, each from a different culture, each from a different country, but both with a common interest that transcended nationalities. He was North American; she was Bolivian. They both were interested in early Bolivian peoples and cultures.

Richard Dawson was a graduate student in anthropology at Case Western Reserve University (CWRU) in Cleveland, Ohio. As his graduate studies evolved, he became interested in physical adaptations to high altitude, an area of research strength at CWRU. His faculty mentors had noted that people indigenous to high altitudes adjusted to the need to offset decreased oxygen in the air they breathed in different ways in the Andes and the Himalayas. The adaptation could be accomplished by altering the oxygen-carrying blood red cells so that they more efficiently delivered the oxygen to body tissues. Or it could be done by altering the lungs so that they provided more oxygen to the blood. In the latter case, changes in the size and configuration of the chest might be expected in response to physical alterations of the lungs. Perhaps both of these adaptations might be found in some people, Richard supposed.

Indigenous people in the Andes had lived at high altitude since prehistoric times. Whatever physical changes in their chest structure had developed in response to altitude might be expected to be present both in modern humans and in prehistoric persons. The latter might be investigated both in skeletal specimens from prehistoric sites and in art from prehistoric cultures. Relevant measurements in contemporary times could be made easily, and it might be revealing to do so both in high altitude-living healthy persons from the general population and patients with chronic lung disease—COPD.

The Instituto de Torax in La Paz, Bolivia, had the facilities to assess modern high altitude dwellers. Richard Dawson hoped to compare data collected there with similar data collected by CWRU faculty members in Tibet. He would also relate his Bolivian measurements to those from the extensive Hamann-Todd collection of skeletons of deceased Ohioans at the Cleveland Museum of Natural History. Clinical diagnosis data were available for that collection, although sparse and often poorly documented.

Dawson had grown up in Shaker Heights, an older but well maintained suburb of Cleveland. His parents were both corporate lawyers, his mother working only part time as she devoted attention to Richard and his two-year-younger sister. They lived not far from Shaker Square, a location that provided access to the rapid transit trains carrying passengers into central Cleveland and the locations of Richard's parents' law offices.

Richard finished third in the class rankings of his graduating classmates from Shaker Heights High School. He continued his education at Northwestern University, and he chose to major in anthropology. He never knew precisely why he chose that major. An interesting lecture early in his sophomore year, perhaps. Once into the subject, however, he found it fascinating. While cultural anthropology and sociology were more popular among his classmates, he found the physical and anatomic aspects of the field most intriguing. Faculty members at Northwestern had developed programs related to the study of Mayan civilizations. They interested him and stimulated him to pursue the field further.

During a summer internship at the Cleveland Museum of Natural History following his junior year at Northwestern, he became aware of the Hamann-Todd skeletal collection. The clinical data relating to these human skeletons was so sparse as to be meaningless, but the specimens themselves were in stable and satisfactory conditions so that they could be measured accurately.

Without knowing precisely when or why the idea pushed itself into his brain, he decided he would like to pursue a graduate program in physical anthropology, relating measurements from the Hamann-Todd collection to those in other cultures. He applied for and was accepted into the CWRU graduate program in anthropology. He found the work of his faculty mentors who were studying adaptations to high-altitude living exciting. With two years of course work and a much labored over thesis proposal behind him, he was now in the high altitudes of the Andes. He was based in La Paz, Bolivia, working with anthropologists at the Universidad Mayor de San Andres. He was carefully photographing and measuring in all dimensions bony specimens from the pre-Incan site, Tiahuanaco, located not far from La Paz on the high intermountain plateau known locally as the Altiplano (high plain). It was there, with calipers and measuring tape in hand, that he met Rosa.

Rosa Mamani was Bolivian. The eldest of three sisters, she grew up in the Sopocachi neighborhood of La Paz. Her father worked at Yacimientos Petrolíferos Fiscales Bolivianos (YPFB), the Bolivian national oil company; her mother had a part-time position at the reception desk of the Hotel Sucre. They lived comfortably, if not affluently. Believing that fluency in English and familiarity with North American customs would be increasingly important in the world, Rosa's parents enrolled her in the American Cooperative School (ACS) with its international student body, many drawn from the families of diplomats. Finishing secondary school, she joined nearly a thousand other students in the first-year class at the Universidad Mayor de San Andres. Unlike most of her classmates, she took her studies seriously and moved on to the very much smaller second-year class after the first year; others repeated the first year, some many times, enjoying the free lodging and student ambiance.

Rosa was popular among her student peers, and she frequently dated. She was not, however, coupled to any of her male friends and refused to make any such commitment.

Rosa was an attractive young woman. Slim and with a good figure, she wore her hair bobbed to just above her shoulders. She smiled readily and laughed frequently. She had studied English from childhood; her parents believed that fluency in that tongue might be important in whatever career she might chose to pursue. In fact, she liked the language with its more richly nuanced adjectives than were found in her native Spanish. At ACS she lived in an English-speaking world, both with respect to teachers and most of her fellow students.

Encouraged by her mother, she sought out local weavers—*tejedoras*—and introduced them to vendors on Calle Sagarnaga and other markets in La Paz. With this new access to marketing of their hand work, the weavers gladly paid her a commission from the sales price. She also was usually able to collect a commission from the vendors.

In the fourth year of her six-year university course, Rosa

became interested in anthropology: the history of the people of Bolivia—her *patria*, her homeland, her people. She became intrigued by the physical adaptations many generations of high-altitude dwellers had made to the decreased amount of oxygen in their inspired air. She changed her enrollment to the medical school, and sought out faculty members at the Instituto de Torax across the road from the medical school. They were currently interested mostly in the enzymatic changes in red cell hemoglobin that facilitated oxygen delivery when its concentration was low. She found one faculty member, Professor Manuel Ortega, however, who was studying the physiques of high-altitude residents and changes in thoracic habitus that he felt were important in high altitude adaptation. His work interested her, and she arranged to join him in some of his studies of specimens from Tiahuanaco. It was in this context that she met Ricardo—Richard.

Richard and Rosa soon became friends. They worked together easily. They chatted, they told jokes, they laughed. In La Paz they found restaurants—the Circulo Italiano became a favorite—and they often spent evenings at *peñas* enjoying Bolivian folk music and local humor. They were soon a couple and recognized as such by their Bolivian coworkers and friends. But not *novios*; that would imply more than they were ready for. At least not yet. Maybe, in fact, they might be *novios*, or might soon become *novios*. That term probably meant something different to each of them. It was often used in Bolivia to denote couples engaged to be married. But not always. Sometimes it meant couples who were significantly attached to one another, but had not yet formalized their relationship. Whatever they might be called, Richard and Rosa were surely in love and comfortable with that.

Christmas was soon to arrive, and Bolivian *Paceñas* (residents of La Paz) were preparing for the holiday. Not with green boughs so identified with yuletide in North America and Europe— evergreens did not grow in the high altitude of La Paz—but with colored-paper streamers and colorfully wrapped candies. Work on Tiahuanaco and specimens from it would cease for the holiday and not resume until the new year. "Let's do something together," Rosa suggested. "Let's go someplace interesting and fun." They talked of many options, and settled on Machu Picchu. For Rosa it would provide another look into her ancestry. For Richard another high-altitude site, a famous one, a place that ought to be interesting.

As they made travel plans, it soon became apparent if not directly addressed that they would travel as a couple. They would hire a taxi to take them to Puno, just inside Peru, where they would spend the night. The night in Puno presented a challenge as they found themselves about to share a bed for the first time. "Okay, Rosalita," Richard said. "I don't usually wear pajamas. In fact, I don't have any with me. I can sleep in my underwear, and if you would like I can manage on the floor."

"No, my friend, I want you in bed with me. I brought a nightgown, but since you won't be wearing pajamas, I won't wear it. And you must take off your underwear."

The night together went well, and at breakfast the next morning they agreed that the arrangement was a good one. Perhaps a long-lasting one, they each mused without saying so. Certainly one that would continue during this trip. Then by train to Cuzco, where they would stop before descending to Machu Picchu.

A tedious, day-long trip in a crowded coach car. The train stopped frequently, and local residents besieged the passengers offering to sell handcrafts and food. Richard and Rosa purchased *salteñas*—small meat pies—for lunch. How many stops did the train from Puno to Cuzco make? They lost count. More than a dozen, maybe twenty. Then, as evening approached, the train descended from the high plateau into the sheltered setting of Cuzco.

At a tourist office they found a brochure for a hostel, where they made themselves comfortable for the night. They spent the next day in Cuzco. "We've come this far we really should take time to see the cathedral and whatever else is close by." The following day they took the train down the Urubamba Valley. Exiting the bus that had carried them up to the inn, they met Marta and Olaf. Chatting, they learned they would be sharing Christmas at the Machu Picchu inn. "How many others will arrive, will spend this holiday there?" Rosa wondered aloud.

CHAPTER SIX

Arthur

RELAXED AND ENJOYING their pisco, the Machu Pic-chu guests were getting acquainted with one another, asking the "Where are you from?" and "Do you know…?" questions that seem expected in such a situation. The liberally-poured pisco facilitated introductions. The setting and the spirit of Christmas Eve combined to encourage friendship among the gathered holiday tourists.

"In the room the women come and go, talking of Michelangelo," Harriet mused, a Yale English class pushing itself into her thoughts. "Here we all are. Why would anyone, any of us, choose to be here at Christmas? Why aren't we all at home with families? I guess we all have reasons, probably all different reasons."

Evening was not yet looming when still another guest arrived. Fernando broke away from the group to greet him. "Welcome to Machu Picchu, *Señor*. You are Arthur Greene, *¿no es cierto?* Your room is ready. When you have registered, I will take your bag upstairs. You might wish to join the other guests. All of them have gathered in the lounge. We are not full because of the Christmas holiday. You are our last guest to arrive today."

"Yes, I will. But I will wash up a bit first. I spent a few busy hours in Ollantaytambo, and I am ready for a drink. Dinner will be when?"

"It can be ready soon. It is usually at six-thirty, but I will tell the cook to hold it until all of the guests are ready to eat. We will have just one seating tonight."

"Good. I'll be down to join the others in a few minutes."

As Arthur started to turn away, Fernando asked, "What were you doing in Ollantaytambo?"

"Oh, government business. U.S. government, I mean, not Peruvian. My job is working to limit the cocaine trade, and some of it seems to originate there. So I chat with local people, buy them some *cerveza*, and try to find out what I can about *cocaineros*—who they are, what might we offer them to induce them to change to some other business. It's really hopeless, I guess, because there is so much profit in moving cocaine northwards."

As Arthur moved away, Fernando wondered about him. What had he done in Ollantaytambo? Fernando had found on his arrival at Machu Picchu that there were opportunities to augment his salary by connecting with the local cocaine traffickers. Had Arthur contacted those in Ollantayambo with whom Fernando worked? Was Arthur a threat to his lucrative cocaine activities there? Or even worse, might Arthur's dealings there lead to the arrest of some of Fernando's friends and cocaine traffic partners? Indeed, might Arthur's meddling threaten him personally? Yes, it would, he believed. Arthur was indeed a threat. Might there be something—anything—he should or could do to mitigate that threat? Could he get rid of Arthur? How might he get rid of Arthur?

Arthur Greene had always been the smartest kid in every schoolroom class. He expected that, as did his parents. It always happened; he was smart. He was also smaller than most of his

schoolmates and thus frequently a victim of playground bullying.
It always happened; he was small. As a junior high school student,
he mustered his courage and asked Eleanor, a classmate, to go
to the movies with him. During the picture he reached over and
took her hand in his. She pulled it away. It always happened; he
was socially inept.

His high school English class read Golding's *Lord of the Flies*.
He identified with Piggy, the inept boy brutalized by the others.
He felt that he was brutalized by his high school classmates.

College at the University of Chicago was easy for him. He
majored in international relations and finished in three years,
graduating with honors. He found a job as a copy editor with the
Chicago Tribune, but left after about eight months. Neither he
nor his boss felt that he was adept at or well suited for that career.
He moved to Washington, D.C., where he found entry-level work
as a political analyst at the State Department. He was well suited
to that position, and was recognized and promoted. Socially, he
continued to flounder. He found a small apartment and lived
alone. He had few friends. He frequently dined on Stouffer's fro-
zen dinners. Lasagna was his favorite. Saturday afternoon opera
broadcasts in a movie theater were his major outings. He especially liked *Carmen*. Easy listening music. But it was the role of
Don José, the spurned lover, that attracted him. He also often
felt spurned. He could identify with Don José.

He was stuffing papers into his brief case at the end of an
afternoon when one of his coworkers approached him at his desk.
"Arthur, I noticed a job posting that I think might interest you.
I've thought about it, but I really think it is more like you than
me. And it has a higher GS rating than what you and I have here.
So more money, I guess."

"Yeah?"

"Yeah. It's an analyst position, but it's at the CIA. Spook

stuff, I guess. Or maybe just boring political analysis. I'm going to apply, but like I said, I think you would have a better shot at it than me. I printed out the posting. Look at it. And the pay grade is pretty good."

Arthur took the printout from his coworker and stuffed it into his briefcase. "Thanks, Jim. Maybe I'll look into it."

Two weeks later Arthur arranged his few personal effects in a cubicle at the CIA and opened a folder of reports he had been asked to review. His first assignment was a test, he supposed. In fact, he was quite sure that a more experienced analyst had already reviewed and analyzed the contents of this folder. He was being evaluated. The report dealt with a security breach in operations in Colombia. Drug traffic was the reason for interest in that country, he supposed. But, he thought, drugs were not the usual province of the CIA—or should not be. While the earlier analyses, which he supposed he was expected to critique, had focused on the cocaine trade, he thought Colombia must be important for other reasons. He put the folder aside to think about later, and turned to other work.

The next morning he carried the challenging reports to his supervisor and suggested, "Could drug money from Colombia be supporting Castro in Cuba? I suppose it could be, maybe is. But then the real question, it seems to me, is how does it, the money, get there, to Cuba? Not as cash," he said. "There's too much, and that wouldn't be secure. Somehow there's a route through the international banking business, and finding and stopping that should be important. You know, I did get into a bit of Latin America stuff when I was studying international relations at Chicago, and I think the banking route is probably through Panama."

"You're new here?" queried his supervisor.

"Yes," Arthur answered. "I, um, yes. Brand new."

"You've come up with just what we have been thinking in

this case. I think we should put you on this full time. How's your Spanish?"

"Spanish? Well, I had some in high school, but I don't remember much. I've never had a reason to use it."

"If you're going to do what I think I might want you to do, you'll need to be pretty fluent. Starting tomorrow you go to the State Department Foreign Service Institute Language School. Full time. Close up your desk here. They will test you—now and as you progress. I don't want to see you until they give you a grade of three."

Arthur worked hard at Spanish. He borrowed CDs and played them at home, repeating the phrases and trying to hone his pronunciation and phrasing. The basic grammar he had learned in school helped; now he had to master the subjunctive tense, a hidden and usually ignored part of English grammar. His vocabulary grew rapidly. He learned that pronunciation was important. *Papá*, with an accent on the last syllable, was the Pope; *papa* with the accent on the first syllable was a potato. The two should not be confused. Three months later he returned to his supervisor. "*Aquí estoy. Listo a viajar a Sud America. Con titulo de tres, casi cuatro.*"

The CIA placed Arthur in the American embassy in Lima, Peru. His earlier comments on Cuba had been forgotten. In Peru he was assigned as a "cultural attaché." There were no public duties associated with that assignment. In fact, his charge was to learn as much as he could about the cocaine trade and develop approaches to limiting it. A plan to stop it was clearly beyond the pale. However, there might be a way to limit it. In fact, Arthur had little personal interest in the cocaine trade. He would do as his superiors asked, but he was not personally concerned. He had never used the drug, but he believed it was probably less harmful than alcohol. Certainly less harmful than tobacco.

He rather easily developed a list of the principal suppliers to the North American market. Peruvian authorities were willing to arrest them, but Arthur thought that was analogous to putting a band-aid on a wound that needed stitching up. Moreover, they would easily bribe their way out of the Peruvian law enforcement system. He would work on developing ideas for a more comprehensive approach. Perhaps one that would reward rather than attempt to punish local *cocaineros*.

He had been in Lima for about nine months and felt he was making progress in his work when he decided to go to Machu Picchu. Doing so at Christmas time would allow him not to interrupt his work. All his coworkers would be off for the holiday. He deserved a break, he felt. He had a further incentive to make this trip to Machu Picchu. He and his CIA colleagues were tracking the cocaine trade to its North American importers. Some of it involved American tourists. Customs officials were alert to that, but there were other aspects of importance. There would be no place better than Machu Picchu to take the measure of typical American tourists in Peru.

There were at least two major facets to the international cocaine commerce. Peruvian entrepreneurs had to organize the local purchase of crude cocaine from *campesinos*. Peruvian exporters then had to organize its shipment northward. Arthur felt that focusing solely on the exporters was a limited strategy that would produce limited results. Somehow one had to remove or reduce the rewards reaped by drug producers.

To explore and learn more about the early steps on the ladder that reached from small *campo fincas* to drug exporters, Arthur would stop in Ollantaytambo on the way to Macchu Picchu. Doing so meant taking a bus down the Urubamba Valley rather than riding the more comfortable tourist train. There were some interesting ruins on terraces rising up steep slopes in

Ollantaytambo. They were generally bypassed by tourists. Arthur knew of but had never visited them. Ollantaytambo was also an important center for the cocaine *negocio*. It was in that connection that he felt he should make this stop, although he doubted that anyone with whom he talked would tell him anything he did not already know. Yet two days in Ollantaytambo might turn out to be two days profitably spent; one could never be sure.

Arthur enjoyed his visit to Ollantaytambo. The ruins were impressive. The town struggled to be a tourist destination. There were tourist amenities—places to stay and to dine—but most tourists eschewed a visit, choosing to go directly to Machu Picchu. Those famous ruins were hard for other sites to compete with.

Arthur arrived in mid-afternoon. He found a room at the Hotel Samanapaq, an upscale tourist hotel. Leaving the hotel, he walked into the center of the town and found a local bar where he bought a *cerveza*. He chatted with the bartender, and on his recommendation sought out a Señor Victor Morales. After talking with him, Arthur concluded that Morales did indeed have an important local role in cocaine traffic and also that Morales would not help him in any effort that might disrupt it. In fact, this conversation had probably guaranteed that no one else would reveal anything important to him. Word spreads quickly in rural communities.

Americans provide the market and incentive to the Peruvian drug producers and merchants who handle the product. Americans distribute cocaine in the U.S. More than that, the tentacles of the American drug world infiltrated and influenced much of its Peruvian aspects. The bodies of those American octopus arms should be within the reach of American law enforcement if solid evidence could be accumulated. Arthur was working with agents of the U.S. Drug Enforcement Agency. The DEA had the authority, although rarely the means, to enforce American drug laws. Arthur felt that the DEA efforts were appropriate, but that they would not be sufficient unless complemented by action at the level of local drug production. Some small part of that local production might be centered in Ollantaytambo, but he would be unlikely to learn much about it during this visit. *Cocaineros* would not reveal much to *norteamericanos*.

Arthur was concerned that there were many casual drug users among American tourists, and some of them smuggled modest amounts of cocaine into the U.S. when they returned from vacation travel in the Andean Region. That activity was not to be ignored, he felt, although his superiors considered it not worth major effort. Other, larger routes of cocaine traffic were more important. To Arthur, however, small details should not be overlooked. He had always been a detail person, a person who saw the "small" as well as the "big" picture. One would see only where one looked, he believed, and he liked to look where others had not.

Movement of large sums of money was involved in the greater cocaine trade, and there must be international routes for that banking commerce. Perhaps Panama, as he had suggested while still in training. Among the money pathways, Arthur had become aware of funds that seemed to be moving through brokerage accounts managed by Ted Hewes. Arthur knew nothing of Hewes, but he had learned that he was booked into the inn at Machu Picchu for Christmas. Combining CIA business with pleasure seemed to Arthur justification for spending the holiday at this famous site in the Andes. He could evaluate Hewes and decide what actions might be appropriate by which law enforcement agencies in Peru or the United States.

Arthur was—had always been—what some would call a nit-picker. Yes, he acknowledged, major emphasis should be

placed on major drug traffickers. However, other drug importers should also be targeted. The solo travelers who took home
a plastic baggie of cocaine did not seem important to many law
enforcers. But to Arthur they reflected a culture that was growing
in America and that should be stamped out wherever it might be
possible to do so. Ignoring them was to ignore the local suppliers
who created the demand.

Arthur's efforts met disfavor not only from travelers who were
stopped at customs to face drug charges but also from Peruvian officials who attempted to do everything possible to promote
tourism in Peru. American tourist dollars were welcome. Programs or actions that targeted or discouraged American travelers
often were not.

With no specific questions or thoughts in his mind, Arthur
asked for and obtained a list of all of the guests who had
reserved rooms at the inn at Machu Picchu. It was the sort of
obsessive-compulsive thing that he often did. He wanted to know
who else besides himself and Ted Hewes might be spending the
holiday there. Interesting people, he thought as he read the information that was provided to him.

The woman and her daughter who had jumped ship in Salaverry caught his attention. They were in Peru without having
passed through immigration. How might they leave the country?
Also bypassing authorities? If leaving by irregular routes, would
they be carrying cocaine? Had this been their plan all along? She
was identified as a travel agent. What might that mean for cocaine
traffic by tourists? Or by others? By business travelers?

The Russian couple purporting to be Swedish and working
in that country's Peruvian embassy. They had come to Arthur's
attention some six months earlier. As far as he knew, they were
not important in the cocaine trade. They might or might not
be casual users themselves, he supposed, but he had been in

conferences at the embassy where their activities as possible Russian spies were discussed. And drug money often supported espionage work in Peru.

The young couple from New York were probably tourists—nothing more. Cocaine users, perhaps, but not otherwise suspect, he supposed. Christmas seemed a strange time to be away from families, however. And the school teacher who planned to walk to the ruins. A holiday school break, he assumed. But also the rainy season in the Andes. Why now rather than in the North American summer, when the mountain ridge trail would be mostly dry?

Then there was the American student traveling with a Bolivian student. His information about those two was limited, but he understood they were both involved in a Bolivian-American cooperative anthropology project of some sort. Both students working on the same project, he supposed.

Musing to himself, Arthur wondered about these American visitors to Machu Picchu. Why were they in Peru at a time when most Americans would choose to be at home with their families? Christmas holidays were not usually times for getaway vacations. What occult agendas did they have?

His baggage stowed in his room, Arthur entered the inn's lounge and poured himself a glass of pisco sour from the pitcher on the bar. Surveying the group, he thought he could identify all of those present. His earlier research had given him fair understanding of these persons with whom he would spend the next two days. He walked across the room to join a group surrounding Ted Hewes. "Good evening," he introduced himself. "I'm Arthur Greene. I live in Lima now, but I'm American. So are most of you, I suppose. I work at the embassy there."

"Oh, welcome," Erica said. "This is Ted." She then introduced the others. "Julia—she's my mother—and I were on a cruise ship and left it to come here. We're from New York. Mark and Harriet are also from the Big Apple." She indicated them with her arm. "We didn't know them there. New York City. It's big. Nobody knows anybody there. Mom works at a travel agency in New York, and so she got us a good deal on the cruise ship. But an interior cabin! I was glad to leave the boat! We stopped in Lima, but I didn't like it. Too much of a big city for me. I get all of that I want back home in New York.

"Rosa and Richard here are anthropologists," she added, turning to the couple. "Rosa is Bolivian and Richard American. They are doing something with bones, I guess. In Bolivia, I think. Is that right?"

"Yes, I suppose so. But it's more about what the bones tell us about the people they came from than about the bones themselves," Richard commented.

"My people, my ancestors," Rosa added. "But we're really just students at this point. We're not yet experts on these matters—or on anything, I guess. And we're here because the university is closed for the holidays and we thought it would be fun to get away. Together," she added with a smile directed at Richard.

Arthur shrugged. Then he commented, "Studies of that type are really a form of exploitation. You should be doing this, yes, but your boyfriend should not. Or he should be teaching you to do it. And do you have a Bolivian professor supervising you?"

"Yes, Professor Ortega," Rosa replied.

"And when Richard publishes his paper, will he be an author, or maybe just a footnote? And you, Rosa, another footnote?"

"Arthur, that's your name, right?" Richard commented. "You may know something about your job at the embassy in Lima, whatever it is or isn't, but you obviously know nothing about the academic world. Rosa's and my names will both be at the top of any publications of our work. Just where Ortega's name will appear can't be decided yet. But it will appear—appropriately. So get off your soap box and stick to whatever you do at the embassy in Lima, if you do anything worth sticking to. Your comments here are inappropriate and not welcome."

There was an awkward silence in the group. Erica spoke up to interrupt it. "And then these folks are Olaf and Marta," she resumed her account. "They're from Lima and are some sort of diplomats. Actually, they're Swedish or Norwegian or something, and they're stationed in an embassy in Lima. Maybe you know them there." In fact, Arthur had met most of the European diplomats in Lima, and he was quite sure that Olaf and Marta were not among them. Embassy workers, perhaps, but not diplomats. Most embassy employees were not. On the other hand, most non-diplomatic embassy personnel were locally hired. Drivers, office workers, and such were too easily hired locally to be imported. Whatever these two said they were, they probably had other substantial and perhaps clandestine roles in their embassy.

"And over here is Charles. He's my hero—my Superman. He walked here from Cuzco. Can you believe that? So that's who we all are.

"And Ted is just showing us a gold figure he picked up at a museum. It's real gold, isn't it?" she asked, turning to Ted.

"Well, I think so. At least it was in the Gold Museum."

"Did you buy it in the shop there?" Arthur asked. "If so, I suspect it is no more than thinly plated brass. But then I'm a natural skeptic about things like that."

"No," Ted replied. "It was in with other exhibits of gold things. Everything was poorly displayed. Just sort of spread around. So I just picked it up and put it in my pocket. Sort of on an impulse."

"You mean you stole it?" Erica asked with surprise in her voice.

"Well, I guess so, technically. But it wasn't part of an organized

Arthur   · 75

display, and there was no one around to ask about it. I think I'll
give it to a museum back home. They'll appreciate it."

"But customs?"

"I'll just carry it in my pocket."

Dismayed, Arthur shook his head. "You stole it!"

Ted shrugged, not revealing his concern that he could find
himself in a Peruvian jail if Arthur or any of the others were
to report his theft. He was not a criminal, and picking up an
unattended small ornament did not seem to him like a major
transgression. What if Arthur pursued his expressed concern?
What could that lead to? He would have to find a way to neu-
tralize this Arthurian threat. Should he—how could he—get rid
of Arthur?

An awkward silence was broken by Harriet, who turned to
Arthur and said, "Tell us what you do. I think I heard you say you
work at the embassy in Lima. The American Embassy, I assume.
Are you some sort of diplomat? Do you issue visas to Peruvians
who want to go to the U.S.?"

"Yes. Well, I do work at the embassy, but I have nothing to
do with visas. And I am not a diplomat." With a grin, he added,
"Lots of the time I think I have nothing to do with anything! I'm
supposed to figure out ways to prevent cocaine from getting into
North America. That should be easy. Right?"

"Well, I guess not," Harriet responded. "So, there are
Peruvians who grow coca in these steep mountain valleys. It's
a profitable crop, a very profitable crop. Could we tell them to
grow something else? There're plenty of North Americans who
have never been to the Andes who seem to think so. Corn or
wheat, maybe? On mountain slopes! Oh, yes. And nothing that
would compete with what we grow in the States, of course. Not
grapes, if those who vote you into office come from California."

"Well, I've thought about this a lot. In the end, I believe, the only possible answer—and maybe it's not really possible—is for Americans, people like you all here in this room, to collectively decide not to use drugs. Well, at least not cocaine. But of course, alcohol is okay and certainly caffeine."

"So why shouldn't we just accept cocaine in America? Like alcohol or coffee?"

"No, Harriet, no. Whether you think cocaine is really bad or just a little bit bad or even okay, you have to realize that the illegal drug trade is bad for America. It spawns crime. And furthermore, cocaine is addictive. Just as many Americans can't do without that morning cup of coffee, cocaine users can't just do without the drug. Maybe we could regulate it in the way we regulate alcohol, but I don't think so. In the end, I have come to think that what we are doing now is about all that we can and should do. Just putting our collective fingers into holes in dikes, if you will. One hole after another and then another and another."

"Hmm...."

"Currently, we, I and the folks I work with, are focusing on tourists who smuggle cocaine back with their luggage. In terms of the amount of drug, that's a small amount. But it is somehow a glamorized amount. You know, 'Look what I got back through customs.' It sort of makes it okay. Maybe legitimizes all the drug trade. It's only wrong if you get caught, you know. That's a very slippery slope. Smuggling cocaine home is never okay. So it's a current thrust for us. And as it happens I seem to be one of the ones assigned to do the thrusting. So if any of you try to take home some cocaine and get caught, you can blame me! And I guess that if I have any reason to suspect that any of you might try to get even a small amount of drug through customs, I'll have to pass that information along. And that might make American immigration and customs ugly for you."

Arthur had somehow climbed upon a soap box he usually

preferred to avoid, especially with a group of people he did not know well. He was about to say more, not knowing just what he might say, when Fernando appeared and announced dinner. That ended his oration. As a group, they all entered the dining room.

As he joined the others entering the dining room, Arthur found himself thinking about his fellow guests. How likely was one of them to try to take cocaine back to the States? Why should they do so if they already had suppliers at home? As some sort of gesture of defiance, perhaps? Was such an attitude behind Ted's theft from the Gold Museum? Or Julia's lack of concern about her illegal entry into Peru? And all of the tattoos he had noticed on Mark? What did they say about him? Rosa was Bolivian. Surely she knew coca, and perhaps had introduced Richard to it. Olaf and Marta seemed settled in Lima, but their story did not seem probable to him. A strange company, he thought. All or most of them potential small-time *cocaineros*.

CHAPTER SEVEN

Fernando

FERNANDO GOMEZ, THE MANAGER of the ridge-top inn at the ruins of Machu Picchu, was actually Bolivian, although he had been in Peru for nine years and had held his present position for nearly four. Born in the central Yungas Valley town of Coroico, he was intelligent and energetic. The Yungas Valley is a fertile agricultural region on the slopes of the Andes Mountains, northeast of La Paz, Bolivia's functional capital. Reached by a tortuous truck-traveled mountain road, it provides produce for La Paz.

Coca is a principal Yungas crop. Grown on terraced slopes, dried on stone patios of haciendas from former days, the leaves are soaked in kerosene to extract the drug. The resultant cocaine-rich mash is shipped out of the valley to *cocaineros* who further extract the drug from it.

Coroico is the commercial center for the Yungas region. It is there that the mountain-conquering road from La Paz divides into routes serving the separate North and South Yungas Valleys. A hospital in Coroico serves the region, and its Hotel Prefectoral provides reasonable rooms and meeting places. Its dining room serves a passable dinner, although menu options are usually limited. As a boy Fernando earned spending money in tips from hotel guests for whom he toted luggage. The Sunday market in Coroico is large and draws residents from much of the region.

Fernando was an intelligent and energetic youngster. Coroico offered primary schooling with teachers usually present. Fernando's parents insisted that he attend classes regularly and monitored his grades. His mother befriended the school's teachers, visiting them at the end of class times and making a point of meeting them on market days and sharing opinions about the produce offered by vendors. She also closely monitored Fernando's school homework and assignments. Although they had had little formal schooling themselves, Fernando's parents believed that education provided opportunity, and they wished that for their son. As a youngster he helped support the family by picking coca leaves.

Encouraged by his father, he had attended the Universidad Mayor de San Andres (UMSA) in La Paz. He was a good student, earning honors. Friendly with his fellow students, he sometimes joined in their frequent *manifestaciones,* protesting local politics, academic rules, or a defeat of the local *futbol* (soccer) team. He eschewed the more aggressive of these student protests, not wanting to join his fellow students facing baton-wielding police officers. By the time Fernando had finished the six-year course at UMSA, he had decided never to return to Coroico. In fact, he had become determined never to look back, a policy that carried him forward to new activities and new venues.

Leaving Bolivia, his home-land, his *patria,* with no regrets, he traveled to Lima, Peru. There he found work at the Grand Hotel Bolivar. Armed with a push broom, he cleaned corridor floors. As he extended his efforts to general cleaning of the hotel's public areas, he became noticed by the manager. Soon he was manning the reception desk, initially at night, then during the busy daytime hours.

Ever alert for opportunities, he noted that a concierge position was open at the Sheraton Hotel down the street. He applied and soon found himself busily advising tourists on the sights of Lima. He enrolled in an evening course in English, the universal language of tourism. He familiarized himself with those parts of Lima that appealed to tourists, including the old central city and also upscale Mira Flores. He collected menus from restaurants in Mira Flores and assembled them in a notebook binder for review by the hotel guests who visited his concierge desk. He enlisted taxi drivers as tour guides, establishing with them fixed-price tours of the city, collecting for himself commissions from the drivers.

Fernando saw a posting for an assistant manager position at the Machu Picchu inn. Without hesitation, he applied. He was accepted three weeks later; in fact he later wondered if there had been any other applicants. He would soon discover that there was no more senior manager. The inn would be his responsibility.

Traveling to his new post, he found the Urubamba valley reminiscent of the Bolivian Yungas. In his new managerial position, he immediately set about suggesting and then making improvements. He obtained local textiles to adorn barren guest-room and public area walls. He found a local carpenter and commissioned him to build bookshelves on the interior wall of the lounge opposite the windows. Lacking books, he placed local ceramics on the shelves. He found a village seamstress to make curtains for the windows in the lounge using local motifs. He approached Humberto, the inn's cook, offering him the title of chef and also challenging him to come up with a menu featuring well-prepared local specialties. He set up a bar in the inn's lobby, stocking it with Argentine whiskies bearing internationally recognizable names, albeit not authentic international products.

The inn prospered under his management. He raised the

room rates by a barely noticeable five percent. He made the dinner menu an *a la carte* one, finding, as he expected, that most guests chose the higher-priced offerings. And the lobby bar took money from the vacationing, not penny-pinching hotel guests. The inn had long offered a buffet lunch for day-tripping visitors to the ruins. He continued that practice, introducing local specialties to the luncheon menu, and making the buffet *a la carte*. Thus it and the inn became more profitable. He was given the title of Senior Manager and a welcomed raise in salary.

Fernando had been an occasional user of cocaine since his boyhood in Bolivia's Yungas, where cocaine was a principal crop. He had connected with a supplier in Lima while working there. Continuing his habit upon leaving Lima, he found a supplier in Ollantaytambo, not far from Machu Picchu. When he discovered that one of his returning inn guests from Chicago was in the business of supplying cocaine to the North American trade, he set himself up as a supplier, carefully not revealing his source in Ollantaytambo. With help from some of his travel industry acquaintances from his days in Lima, he was able to establish reasonably secure routes for moving the drug from Peru to Chicago. Later he was able to connect with other guests and expand his operations to California and New York City.

The extra income this trade brought to him was welcome. Always discrete, he had no personal moral concerns with the drug. His cocaine use had not damaged his life or the lives of most of the Yungas dwellers of his youth. That American agents tried to interfere with and suppress the cocaine trade annoyed him, but he and his Peruvian colleagues were reasonably adept at avoiding them. He would have to be careful, however, with Arthur Greene, his soon-to-arrive guest who was employed at the American embassy in Lima and, he supposed, might be working as part of the North American effort to suppress cocaine traffic.

CHAPTER EIGHT

Dinner

THE GROUP MOVED TO the dining room. Marta took Olaf's arm and held him back. "We have to be careful here, Olaf. This guy, Arthur, says he's after small-time cocaine traffickers. That's us. If he finds out what we do, what we're doing, we could be in trouble."

"Yeah, but he won't. We're okay. Just relax and enjoy dinner. There's nothing to worry about. Nobody here is going to suspect us of anything. In fact, my guess is that nobody here cares at all about what we do or don't do. Or what anybody else does, really. Except Arthur, the new guy, I suppose. But he's also on holiday. It's Christmas Eve, after all."

"Don't be so sure, Olaf. This Arthur guy's business is looking for people like us. If he figures us out, we could be in big trouble. We could well be back in Sweden—if we're lucky. Or maybe a Peruvian jail. I don't like this guy. Think about it. How could we silence him? Maybe he should be sacrificed to an Inca god!"

"Okay. Okay. But for now, let's enjoy dinner."

Somewhat behind the others, Rosa and Richard moved to the dining room. "Arthur isn't making any friends tonight, is he," Rosa commented.

"He sure isn't. I wonder what got into him. Too much pisco, or is he always like this? Well, anyway, we're not in the cocaine business."

"No, but as a student, I've tried it," Rosa added. "Haven't you?"

"Nope. It's not very common among students in the U.S. More marijuana. Probably about the same. It doesn't do much for me. I prefer beer."

"Not *chicha*?" Rosa teased.

"Yuck!"

"Anyway," Rosa continued, "we have to be careful about Arthur. He could be a big threat to us. He's in the American embassy in Lima, but I'd be pretty sure he has friends in the U.S. embassy in La Paz. All those diplomats interact. I don't like him. He could make trouble for us if he wanted to. And he seems pretty unfriendly this evening. I wish he weren't here."

Harriet spoke up. "Look. Let's push all these tables together. There are only eleven of us—well, maybe we should include Fernando and make it twelve—so let's all sit together at one table." She moved to start rearranging tables and was quickly joined by Charles.

With tables rearranged, they took their places. Couples sat together. Ted took the seat at the head of the table. It seemed natural to him to do so, and somehow it seemed appropriate to the others. Or at least, they accepted it. The others took places along the sides. Seated next to Charles, Arthur sat at the end. That's where he belonged. At the end of the table. It always happened.

Fernando, now wearing an apron, assumed the role of *Maître d'*. He passed out printed menus to the seated guests. With appropriate flourishes, he placed napkins over the ladies' laps. "Tonight we have *Milanesa*," he told the diners.

"How about the trout on the menu?" Mark asked. "Is it from Lake Titicaca? And how fresh is it?"

"No. No trout. Tonight we have *Milanesa.*"

"What's that? What's *Milanesa*?"

"That'll be a cutlet of some sort," Charles offered. "It's commonly an entrée in *campesino* restaurants. That's what there is tonight, right?" Charles asked Fernando.

"*Si, Señor,*" Fernando replied. Then he addressed the group. "It's Christmas Eve, so we have only one cook here tonight, and *Milanesa* is all that he has prepared. It will be ready shortly, and I will serve you."

"A veal cutlet?" Ted queried.

"Not likely," Charles interjected. "You should know that. You were a Peace Corps volunteer in Bolivia, after all. What did you get then? '*Carne buena,*' I guess, whatever that turned out to be at the time."

"*Carne Buena* means good meat in Spanish," Rosa pointed out. "But that literal translation isn't right. Or not exactly right. It means better quality meat, I guess. Nothing to do with whether the meat is spoiled or not. For that you have to trust the vendor—or maybe your nose! But if you're buying meat from local markets, the real thing to ask is how old it is. Meat has to be aged. My mom always keeps meat from the market in the bottom of the refrigerator for several days before cooking it."

"I don't know what we have or how well it has been aged," Fernando said. "It's whatever Humberto, the cook, purchased in the market yesterday."

"Goat, perhaps—maybe probably," Charles said. "Lots of goat is eaten in the Andean regions. It should be okay. Just enjoy it and don't ask too much about it. Goat is not too much different from lamb—or from mutton, actually. And better than llama—not as tough."

"I'm sure we'll find it delicious," Harriet commented, apparently hoping to defuse a potentially irksome situation.

"How about wine?" Ted asked. "Do you have a wine list?"

"Yes, of course," Fernando replied. He retrieved the wine list from a sideboard and presented it to Ted.

"I'm not sure what wine is proper with goat meat," he said to the group, "but I think a red would be right for Christmas. Okay, everyone?" There were a couple of nods, but no other responses. Ted's fellow guests had realized what Ted should have known but somehow failed to understand. Dinner tonight would be what the cook had prepared and Fernando served. The entrée would be a *Milanesa*. Wine would be what was on hand.

"I see you have a California cabernet," Ted said to Fernando. "Is it from Napa?"

"Napa? Where is that? I only know what is there on the list."

"Napa is a wine-growing region in California," Harriet said to Fernando.

"Well, I guess we'll chance it. Bring us two bottles of this red." Ted pointed to one of the listings on the wine list. "Put them on my account."

"*Si, Señor.*"

Ted addressed the group. "I shouldn't be surprised, I guess. After all, like Charles, I served with the Peace Corps in the Andes. In Bolivia, actually. Just next door, really. But somehow…" Ted paused, then continued, addressing the group but no one person. "You know, this is a tourist place, and it ought to be well enough run to satisfy tourists. We should be able to order whatever is on the menu and whatever is on the wine list. In Bolivia, we used to say, '*Asi es Bolivia.*' 'This is how it is in Bolivia'—at least it was. But Peru is supposed to be more…well, more something or other, than Bolivia. Especially since this is a tourist Mecca. Anyway, I guess we'll try this cabernet wherever it's from."

Rosa shook her head. "I'm sorry you didn't like Bolivia. It's a good country, and if you'll come there, I'll find good wine for you. Wine from Chile or Argentina."

Presently Fernando returned to report that the inn did not have the wine Ted had ordered. In fact, Fernando told Ted, the only red wine they had, and the only available wine, red or white, was a single bottle of local Peruvian wine. He held out the bottle. "It's old, but I think it still should be good," Fernando reported. "I guess we should have other wines. From Chile, maybe. But we don't. And there is only this one bottle."

"Jesus, Christ," Ted exclaimed. "What sort of dump is this?" He stood up, pushing his chair back. He threw his napkin on the table and walked out. As the other guests watched him, he returned to the lounge, filled a glass from the remaining pitcher of pisco sours, and walked out the front door of the inn.

An embarrassed silence was broken by Julia, who turned to Fernando. "I'm sorry, we're all sorry, for his behavior. Too much pisco, maybe. But he's gone now, so we'd like to get on with dinner. We'll enjoy whatever the cook has prepared. And I think we would like some wine. Again, whatever you have will be fine. We all can share a little from that one bottle."

"Thank you, *Señora*. You are very kind. The cook and I, we will do our best for you."

As dinner concluded, Fernando cleared dishes to the sideboard. While doing so, he addressed the group. "If I may, I'd like to tell you a little about the Inca ruins here."

"Oh, please do," Erica replied with interest and enthusiasm. "And tell us about yourself."

"Well," Fernando began, "I'm actually Bolivian, not Peruvian. I grew up in Coroico, a town in the Yungas region over the mountains from La Paz."

"I've been there. It's a nice place," Rosa interjected. "But I like Chulumani better. The Motel San Antonio there has a nice swimming pool."

"So have I," added Charles. "I stayed in the Hotel Prefectoral in Coroico. And I was there for the Sunday market, which was lots of fun."

"Really?"

"Yes, really. But that's a long story. So, Fernando, tell us your story. It's more important than mine. You come from Bolivia. Are you Quechuan?"

"*Si, Señor.* Yes, I am. Most of the people in the Yungas, where I grew up, are Quechuan. Our heritage is that, but the language is pretty much forgotten. We speak Spanish now. The conquistadores imposed that on us. Of course, the Incas replaced our original Aymara language with their Quechua when they conquered our Bolivian ancestors."

"My family is Quechuan," Rosa interjected. "But I grew up in the city, in La Paz."

"Well," Fernando continued, "I left Coroico and went to the university in La Paz, the functional capital of Bolivia. It's located on Avenida Arce, the Prado. The students there are liberal—maybe all students everywhere are liberal—and there are many manifestations or demonstrations that interrupt the academic programs. Che Guevara is the hero of the students. He was a Bolivian who later joined the Cuban revolution. Then he returned to Bolivia and thought he would give the land back to the farmers who lived on it. But he didn't know the history or the local situation. In the 1950s President Barrientos had already vanquished the big land holders and given their farms back to the people. They owned their farms. They had no interest in Guevara and his give-back-the-land ideas. So the army put a price on his head, and a local resident turned him in and collected the reward. He was shot as he sat drinking coffee. That way the army got rid of him without the fuss and spectacle of a public trial."

"Yes, I know that story," Charles interjected.

"Che was a hero for students," Rosa added, "but it never made sense to me. And most of the students I know have no interest in Che."

Fernando continued his story. "The university is a six-year-long course. I studied business and accounting. After finishing at the university I set out to make a living for myself. I didn't go back to Coroico. I came to Peru and worked in the Grand Hotel Bolivar in Lima. That was okay. I liked that hotel. It's older than the Sheraton, for example, but it has a distinguished atmosphere, if I can put it that way. And the restaurant is good. If your trip takes you back to Lima, I recommend it. I worked hard, and I was promoted. Then I moved to the Hotel Sheraton.

"One day I saw a posting for this job, here at Machu Picchu. It seemed like a good position, and it paid more than I was earning in Lima. So I applied. And here I am. But that's not what I want to tell you about. I should tell you about Machu Picchu.

"It's called 'The Lost City of the Incas,' and the valley 'The Sacred Valley,'" Fernando continued. "Hiram Bingham 'found it,' they say. That's all tourism nonsense, of course. Machu Picchu was never lost, and there never has been anything sacred about the river valley. Everyone who lived near here knew about the ruins. They sit high up on the ridge, and are made of the same stone as the mountain. So it all blends in. If you don't know about it, you can look up and not realize what's here. The Spaniards were all around here after they conquered the Incas in Cuzco. They came down this valley, but they never looked up. Or didn't see the ruins, if they did. Anyway, Hiram Bingham was looking for Incan ruins. He talked to the local folks here, and they told him there were ancient ruins. He was an archeology professor from Yale. That's a university in America."

"Yes," Harriet commented. "A famous one. My husband and I studied there."

"So," Fernando continued, "this Bingham person gave a local boy a coin to show him ruins, and the boy brought him here.

"Okay. This is what I know about the Incas here at Machu Picchu. But there's more to the story of the Incas. And, as I told you, I'm Bolivian, not from Peru, so what I know may not be quite right. Anyway, this is what I know—or think I know. Inti was the Sun God and he came from the *Isla del Sol*, the Island of the Sun, in Lake Titicaca. When I was at the university, I took a trip to Copacabana, the Bolivian city on the northern half of the lake. Some Bolivians say the well-known Brazilian city was named after this one, but I think that it was more likely the other way around.

"Also in Copacabana there is a cathedral with a famous black virgin. Many pilgrims go to Copacabana to light a candle and pray to the black virgin. And there are steps marking the stations of the cross going up a hill. The view from the top is magnificent—the lake and the Isla del Sol."

"Yes," Rosa commented. "Copacabana is very important. I have never been there but I want to go and see the black virgin. All Bolivians should."

"The island is important, because that's where Inti came from. The most impressive thing there is the ancient steps. I don't know how old they are, but it must be more than a thousand years. You can hire a boat to take you out to the island to see the ancient steps.

"Anyway," Fernando continued, "Inti left Lake Titicaca, went to Cuzco, and made himself the first emperor of the Incas. Not him, but someone later on in the Incan dynasty, built Machu

Picchu. Why, no one knows. A fort, a retreat of some sort, an outpost? But it's here, and you should enjoy it.

"So Bingham came here, and then lots of other archeologists. Finally the Peruvian government stepped in and tried to preserve it. And to get as many tourist *soles* out of it as they could. So this hotel was built and everything was done to encourage tourism."

"And we're all tourists here today, and we want to see it," Harriet interjected.

"Yes, yes, you should. So let me just tell you a little about what's out there. And then you should go see the ruins. It's still light enough. You can go out and wander around while I clean up the dishes. Then you can come back for more pisco, if you like. We don't have any fancier after-dinner drinks. And tomorrow go back again. It will be Christmas. There won't be any other tourists, I think. The busses won't run, and maybe not the train. You should have the ruins to yourselves.

"As you approach the entrance to the ruins, you will meet a man dressed so as to look authentically Incan with a couple of llamas. He's always there and ready for you to take photos and give him tips. Or maybe sometimes his brother. Maybe not at Christmastime, however. Anyway, you enter the ruins through a stone doorway. Stop and look at it; don't just rush in. Most tourists do, and they miss something amazing. Perfectly shaped stones. Symmetrical. Fitting tightly together. They did this with no metal other than perhaps copper. They placed the massive lintel stone at the top of the doorway, got it up somehow. It fits perfectly. You will be awed. Once in among the ruins, there's lots to see, although many tourists just rush ahead to see the famous sundial without bothering to look at what's around them.

"There's a courtyard of sorts with three windows that look out over the Urubamba Valley. It's important and special, I think. Maybe some sort of ceremonial place. Again you will be amazed at the stone work done with only primitive tools and no hard metal. The Temple of the Sun is impressive. It's round, which is unusual, I think. There's a stone stairway leading up to it.

"Take time to look at the water collection system they built. All they had was rain water, no wells. Of course, it rains a lot here, but they needed to collect the rain water to drink and for cooking. Nobody knows how many people were here or for how much time, but they must have needed water.

"There are less elaborate ruins along the south side. Housing for workers, for ordinary people, I think. At least that's what the guides tell tourists, although they don't really know. Nobody really knows.

"Then there's Intihuatana, the famous 'sun dial.'"

"What's that?" Julia asked. "Does it tell time?"

"Well, that's what it's called. And no, it doesn't tell time. It's a big flat stone. At one end of it there are a couple of steps up to its flat surface. It has sort of a pillar or post sticking up from one side. All part of the same big stone. Amazing; I can't imagine how it was created without stone-carving tools. Maybe that pillar-like projection could cast a shadow or something. It probably does. But I really don't think that stone was a sun dial that could tell time. Like much of what is here, no one really knows. But tourists want answers. So we speculate. But how it was carved is what intrigues me. The only metal they had to work with was copper, which is too soft to cut stone.

"Supposedly the Inca priests tied the sun to this stone. So at equinox times, they could start pulling the sun back from where it had moved. At least, that's what the tour guides tell visitors. But of course, like things about most of what is here, and as I said, nobody really knows. But it is an interesting stone carved into shape with nothing but copper tools and other stones. The tour guides make it the dramatic end of their tours. You know, where

they put out their hands for tips and tell the tourists they are free
to wander on their own."

"So the tour guides can hustle back and collect another group
of moneyed tourists?" Mark asked.

"Of course."

"Let's go out and see the ruins," Harriet said to her husband
as they pushed their chairs back from the table. "That's why we're
here."

"No!"

"No? Why not?" Harriet looked and was reassured that the
other guests had moved out of the dining room. If she and Mark
were going to squabble, she would prefer to have their altercation
privately.

"Look. You brought me here to get me away. To get me off
drugs, although this place is close to a center of cocaine production. Anyway, I'm glad you did. It's an interesting place. But top
of my agenda is that I need to quit cocaine. It isn't easy. At the
moment, I just don't feel right. Somehow, I'm not myself. I'll get
there, but I'm not yet clean, if you want to say it that way. Not
yet. I'm still a junkie. And right now I don't feel good. I feel sort
of strange. Maybe part of my drug withdrawal, I guess."

"Oh, Mark, I know it's tough for you. I know what you're going
through—or at least I know it's real hard for you. But come with
me and enjoy this place while were here. Let's do it together."

"No. Not tonight. I can't. Maybe tomorrow. I think I should
go to bed now." He turned away from Harriet and walked toward
the stairs. He paused, turned, and once more addressed his wife.
"You know, that Arthur guy bothers me. A lot. I think he believes
I'm a cocaine trafficker. One of the small-timers he said were his
current project. I worry that he might want to turn me over to
Peruvian drug authorities. That could be a real disaster. I want
to get clean, but I have to stay out of trouble to do it. Somehow

Arthur threatens me. He could make big trouble for me, I think. I wish he wasn't here. I wish he would just disappear somehow. I wish I could get rid of him. I really don't like him being here.

"As I said, Harriet, I'm really and truly glad you brought me here and away from New York," Mark continued. "Getting me away was smart. And the only hope for getting me clean. But it isn't easy for me. Tomorrow I should be better, I hope. So you go. Join some of the others. Make some sort of excuse for me. I'll turn in. Or maybe I'll wander about on my own. I probably will. I'm really not sleepy."

As Harriet stood pensively in the hall, Julia approached her. "Should we go out and see the ruins together? It's a lovely evening."

"Oh, yes. Let's do. That's a lovely young woman, Erica, your daughter."

"Thanks. She has turned out well."

"Her father?"

"Long since gone. She never knew him, which is just as well. A college romance, actually. Nothing more than that. My dad wanted me to get an abortion, but I wanted a child—my child."

"Ted seemed to be paying quite a bit of attention to her. But he's old enough to be her father, it seems to me."

"I guess. Anyway, she's now of an age when young men are buzzing around. Like bees around a honey pot or tomcats round a female puss in heat, I warn her. Maybe Ted wishes he were younger than he is. And if he oversteps, I'll deal with him. Harshly if necessary. I can do the protective 'Momma Bear' act pretty well. "

"I'm not there yet. Someday, I hope. But I hear you, and I'm with you. Predatory older men should be lined up against a wall and shot. Isn't that what Eliza Doolittle wanted to do with Henry Higgins?"

Julia linked her arm in Harriet's, and the two women moved toward the door heading for a stroll through the ruins. As the two women moved out, Fernando waved to them. "Enjoy the ruins. It's a lovely night."

"Oh, yes, we will."

Hand in hand, Rosa and Richard crossed the front hall and headed for the door and the ruins. "Fernando," Rosa said, "you have so much to do. Don't you ever get to enjoy the ruins?"

"Yes, I'm busy tonight, because it's only me and Humberto, the cook, here now. But I'll finish here soon. Then I think I'll go out there while it's still light. I love these ruins. When the inn is busy I can't get out to enjoy them. But tonight, I'll be done here soon and go out there."

"We'll see you there and look forward to a guided tour."

Leaving the inn, they met Harriet and Julia and walked with them to the ruins. Slowly the four tourists wandered the site, stopping frequently. They passed the sundial stone with its vertical projection, but wondered if it really was a sundial. Unlikely, they thought.

"This place truly deserves its 'World Heritage' designation," Harriet commented.

While others were touring the ruins, Arthur wandered into the lounge where he joined Charles at the bar. "There's some Scotch here, probably from Argentina," Charles offered. "Whatever the label says, most international brands of liquor in this region come from Argentina."

"Thanks." Arthur accepted a generous tot from Charles.

"Your job at the embassy is to find ways to keep cocaine from entering the U.S.?"

"Yeah. And these days I'm focused on casual travelers who think there's nothing wrong with smuggling in small amounts. And maybe there isn't, except that the little amounts get bigger and bigger. And once addicted, a person is hooked and can't stop. And needs more. And more. And will do what is needed to get it—anything."

"So it's people like the folks here tonight that you're after?"

"Yeah, among others, if they buy cocaine here in Peru and try to take the drug through customs. I don't know if any of these folks here with us would do that. They're pretty much ordinary tourists. But you never know.

"Sometimes I feel like I can't do anything," Arthur continued. "Why try? There really is no way to stop casual use of cocaine and its import. Once not so long ago cocaine use was accepted. Sherlock Holmes. Remember? He had his seven-percent solution that he injected himself with. How harmful is it really, I ask myself. Maybe we should treat cocaine like alcohol and legalize it but hope to control it. I guess that's a slippery slope, however, and nobody else in the world has legalized it, really. So, I do what I can do, hoping maybe I make a difference somehow, but not really believing that I can."

"I guess that's what we all do—hope to make a difference. Certainly that's what I hope with my students," Charles commented.

"What difference?" Mark asked as he entered the lounge. "Can I join you?" he asked, reaching for the whiskey bottle.

"We're talking about cocaine traffic and addiction," Arthur responded. "It's my job to try to stop it, but it really is a hopeless challenge."

"I know, I know," Mark commented. "I was a user, an addict. And it destroyed my life. I lost my good job. And I got these stupid tattoos. He held out his arms. But I'm clean now, and Harriet brought me on this holiday to keep me away from frustrating encounters with family that might have made me lose control. I guess she didn't realize she was bringing me to a place where cocaine is produced. Anyway, I am drug-free, and I plan to stay that way."

"I hope so," Arthur commented. "But what you have just told me, I'll have to pass on. And that means you are going to get thoroughly searched at customs when you head back. Your bags will be opened and you may be strip-searched. Both you and Harriet. Sorry, but that's my job."

"Really! You assume I will try to smuggle cocaine in? What kind of an ogre are you? What happened to presumption of innocence? Isn't that the law?"

"You just told me you were an addict."

"Yeah, I was. But not now."

"Sorry, but in this business, addicts don't stop using."

"Well I have, and your assumption that I can't leave drugs behind is unwarranted. More than that, it's insulting, demeaning. And somehow threatening. I'm not your ordinary back-alley druggie. Nor am I a modern, hip guy who thinks drugs are okay. I was hooked—an addict. But no more. Thanks to lots of help from my wife who brought me here, I'm drug-free. And I'll stay that way. I really will. So you're not winning any friendship gold stars with me tonight. I don't like you and your unnecessary threats. You're just making me very angry at you!" Mark's voice had risen almost to a shout.

Hoping to defuse this potentially incendiary conversation, Charles put down his glass. "Let's join the others in the ruins. It's still light, and those ruins are the reason we're here—we very motley bunch of Christmastime tourists."

Outside the inn, Charles pulled Mark aside, leading him a short distance down the access road and away from the ruins. "Take it easy with what you say to Arthur, would you? He's out to suppress all cocaine traffic, even casual. You're just going to guarantee that all of us will be suspected of drug smuggling when we reenter the U.S. You've already done it for yourself. You and Harriet are going to have an unpleasant journey through customs. I hadn't really thought about it, but it would be pretty easy for me to pay for this way-over-budget vacation by taking in a little cocaine."

"Would you?"

"Hmm. I hadn't thought about it. But it wouldn't be hard to do. Of course, I'd have to get rid of Arthur first. Maybe I should do that."

CHAPTER NINE

The Body

THE INN GUESTS WERE assembling for breakfast in the dining room, finding the places they had occupied at dinner. As he poured coffee, Fernando addressed them. "*Huevos reveltos con salchicha*, scrambled eggs with sausage, is what we have this morning."

"*No hay tocino*, no bacon?" Charles asked.

"No, only sausage."

At that point Erica burst through the front door of the inn and ran into the dining room. "It's Arthur. Out there in the ruins. On the altar stone. He's dead!"

"What!"

"Yes, he's on his back on the altar stone, and there's a knife sticking out of his chest." Pushing back their chairs, all of the breakfasters rose and, in a troop, followed Erica to the ruins. Fernando joined them. As Erica had promised, they found Arthur lying on his back atop the altar stone. The handle of a large kitchen knife protruded from his chest, the blade presumably having pierced his heart.

"Don't touch anything," Ted commanded. "Fernando, call the police."

"I will try, but this is Christmas, a holiday."

"Well, tell them this is a murder. And if they can't come right away, we should put a sheet over him before some birds get to him."

"Oh, God," Harriet said, tears running down her face.

CHAPTER TEN

Captain Ruiz

BACK IN THE LOUNGE of the inn, the subdued company gathered, but said little to one another. That one of them was a murderer was distressingly evident, although unsaid. Fernando had gone out again and covered Arthur's body with a sheet. He joined the group. "I put a sheet over the body so as to keep the birds away from it. I have called the police. They will come, but it may be some time before they arrive."

"We'll be here," Julia commented. "There's no place else to go, and probably no way to get anywhere on Christmas."

"Yes, *Señora* Young. Is there anything I can get for you? Or do for you?" Fernando replied. "Or for anyone?"

"I guess not," Julia said. "I don't want any more breakfast. Does anyone?" she asked turning to address the other members of the group. There were a few shaken heads, but no reply. "Thank you, Fernando."

"I think it will be the afternoon before the police arrive. Lunch will be ready at noon."

"Yes, thank you."

Five or ten minutes passed in silence. Then Mark spoke up, turning to his wife. "We came here to see these ruins. There's nothing much else we can do until the police arrive. Harriet, let's go out and walk around the place."

"Yes. Let's do that. But stay away from the sun dial."

"Us too. Can we come with you?" Richard interjected.

"Of course." Hand in hand, the two couples strolled out to the ruins, parting as they entered. The others followed, not as a group but singly and in pairs. Their paths diverged, all avoiding the murder site, however.

"How about climbing Huayna Picchu?" Erica asked her mother.

"Oh, no. Not today. I couldn't concentrate enough to stay on that narrow mountain trail. Another day, but not today. I wonder how long we'll be stuck here. I'm ready to leave now."

"Oh, come on, Mom. Let's give it a try."

"Well, okay. But take it slowly. And I get to turn back if I want to." The two women started slowly up narrow trail. "Now, this is enough," Julia said.

"Okay. It is kinda steep and narrow."

Erica and Julia returned to the lodge in time for a lunch served by Fernando. They ate little, joining their fellow guests in finding they had little appetite. Finishing the meal, they returned to the lounge in time to greet an arriving Jeep bringing three police officers from Ollantaytambo. Fernando greeted them and introduced the guests to them.

"Good afternoon, I am Captain Ernesto Ruiz. My colleagues are Officer Pérez and Officer Martinez. We will first inspect the victim and the murder site. Then we will want to talk to each of you. Can you provide us with a room?" he asked Fernando.

"Certainly. You can use one of the empty guest rooms on the second floor. I will bring extra chairs into one of the larger ones."

"As soon as we have finished inspecting the murder victim and the surrounding area, Officer Martinez will take the body back to Ollantaytambo. Officer Pérez will stay with me here to begin our investigation and to interview each of you.

"We will search each of your rooms. We will try not to disturb your things, but it is the normal routine in a murder case such as this. Of course, the murder weapon seems obvious, so we are not looking for that. Meanwhile, you are all to remain downstairs here in the lounge until we call you to be interviewed. Please, stay here; do not go out to the ruins.

"*Señor* Gomez," Ruiz said addressing Fernando, "I will need your guest list and registration cards. And," he said addressing the group, "each of you must bring your passport when Officer Pérez and I interview you."

The three officers left the inn to inspect the murder site in the ruins.

"This is odd," Martinez said. "He's been stabbed through the heart, but there is no blood! Let's look around. Maybe he was killed elsewhere and carried here after he was dead."

The police officers carefully searched the ruins, but found no blood and no signs of a struggle. They walked slowly back to the inn. "Hah," said Pérez. "Look at this." He held up a length of rope that he found on the ground near the inn. "I think he was strangled with this. The murderer came up behind him, threw this rope over his head, and pulled it tight around his neck. I suspect he was already dead when he was stabbed. That's why he didn't bleed."

Returning to the lounge after inspecting the body and murder site, Ruiz told the group, "It appears that the victim was first strangled, probably with a cord tossed over his head and then pulled tight. He was probably dead when he was stabbed."

"Does that suggest who might have done it, who could have done it?" Harriet asked.

"No, *Señora*, I'm afraid not. But I assure you, we will find out who murdered this man. Do any of you have questions before we start our interrogations?" There were no responses from any of the guests.

"Very well, then. *Señorita* Erica Young," Ruiz continued, "You discovered the body. Correct?"

Erica shut her eyes for a moment. Opened her mouth and closed it.

"Correct?" Ruiz repeated.

"Yes," Erica replied.

"Then we would like to talk to you first. Please come upstairs with me."

Erica rose. So also did Julia. "I'm her mother. I'll come too."

"No, *Señora*. We will talk with your daughter alone."

"But..."

"Alone."

Julia sat down. Erica followed Ruiz up the stairs. She accompanied Ruiz and Pérez into the room they had chosen for their investigation.

"*Bueno, entonces,*" Ruiz opened the conversation. "Now then, *Señorita*, we will ask you some questions. We are not accusing you, you understand. But you discovered the body. The body of Arthur Greene, correct?"

"Yes," again hesitatingly.

"We want you to tell us about it. It was early morning. Before breakfast, correct?"

"Yes."

"And what were you doing out in the ruins at that early hour?"

"Well, I was awake. And up and dressed. And no one else was up. Except Fernando. He was setting the table for breakfast, I guess. So I waved to him, 'Good morning,' and went out. It was a beautiful morning. The sun was just up and there were no clouds. A bright blue sky." Erica realized she was saying more than she needed to. She probably should just answer questions "yes" or "no." Why was she nervous?

"And then you found the victim?"

"Yes" she said. Then she added, "I was walking up the slope towards the altar stone. Past the place where there are those three windows. And then I saw the altar stone. And there was something on it. And when I got closer I saw it was Arthur—with a knife sticking out of his chest. It was awful. I was scared. So I ran back to the inn where everyone else was eating breakfast."

"And then the others followed you out to see the body?"

"Yes."

"All of them?"

"Yes, and Fernando, too."

"Did anyone touch the body? Or the knife?"

"No, we all stood back. And then Fernando got a sheet to cover Arthur's body. He was concerned birds might get to it. Uggh!" Erica shuddered.

"Well now, *Señorita* Young, it seems apparent that one of the guests here killed *Señor* Greene. Do you have any thoughts about who that might have been?"

"No."

"Did no one have a fight or even a disagreement with him?"

"No…. Well, Ted Hewes and he had some disagreement concerning a small gold figure that Mr. Hewes stole from a museum. But that didn't seem very much—certainly not enough to lead to a murder."

"*Señor* Hewes stole a gold figure from a museum?"

"Yes. He said so. I don't know…. I guess you'll have to ask him, if that seems important."

"*Señorita* Young, what is your occupation?"

"I'm a student. At a university—full time. Except for summers, when I have found odd jobs. A shipping room clerk, one summer. A waitress at a Catskills Mountain resort another summer. And Christmas holiday breaks, which is how I could travel here."

"You are not married?"

"No."

"Engaged? Betrothed?"

"No."

"Did you know any of the other guests at the inn before you arrived here?"

"No. Except my mother, of course."

"You did not know *Señor* Greene before meeting him here."

"No."

"That will be all, *Señorita* Young. If we need to ask you anything more, we will summon you again. Now I want to talk to your mother. Will you ask her to come up here, please?"

Downstairs, Erica shrugged and then told her mother to go up to be interviewed.

"Was it bad—uncomfortable?" Julia asked her daughter as she moved to the stairs.

"No. Just simple questions."

Julia ascended to the second floor interview room. "Good afternoon, *Señora* Young. May I see your passport, please?"

"Am I being accused of anything? Do I need an attorney present? That's my right, isn't it."

"No, *Señora* Young. You are not accused. We simply have some questions and hope you might help us with some answers as we try to figure out what happened. Of course, if you want a lawyer, you can hire one—but I don't think you'll be able to find one today here in Machu Picchu. And you understand that you are in Peru and that our laws apply. But we are simply asking questions to find out what happened. That's all. Neither you nor your daughter is accused of anything."

"Yes, of course. I'm sorry. But this whole affair has made me and everyone here, I guess, upset and worried. One of us is a murderer. Not me, but I know I must be on your very short list of suspects. There are only ten of us—eleven if you count Fernando, and Humberto, the cook would make twelve, I guess."

"Of course. Now let me ask you a few questions. When was the last time you saw *Señor* Greene alive?"

"Well, at dinner last night. Maybe for a short time afterwards and before all of us seemed to head out to the ruins."

"Do you have any reason to think that any of the guests here might have had a reason to kill *Señor* Greene?"

"No. He told us he worked at the American embassy and somehow he seemed critical of everyone else—of all of us. He had something to do with cocaine traffic to North America. I suppose some of us have used cocaine. In fact, I have, a bit. Only a few times, actually. But I don't think any of us here are in the cocaine trafficking business. Isn't that mostly done by Peruvians, anyway? I suppose with a U.S. connection on the other end. I'm just an office worker. I'm not a drug smuggler."

"And at what kind of office do you work?"

"A travel agency."

"So, couldn't that offer opportunities for getting drugs into your country?"

"Well, maybe, somehow, I guess. But I have never tried to do anything like that. I just help people plan travel and book airline reservations. " Julia had no intention of revealing the fact that she had facilitated the travel of "mules" carrying cocaine into North America. That could hardly be relevant to the current investigation.

"I see you entered Peru illegally," Ruiz said as he thumbed through the pages of Julia's passport. He handed her passport back to Julia.

"What?"

"There is no entry stamp."

"Well, I guess, maybe. We were on a cruise ship that stopped at Salaverry so tourists could see the ruins at Chan Chan. We got off and saw the ruins with the others, but then we didn't go back to the ship. We spent a night in Trujillo and went to Lima. I knew about Machu Picchu, and I wanted to come here and bring Erica here. We flew to Cuzco, but LAN lost our luggage. And then we took the train here."

"*Señora*, you are likely to have a great deal of difficulty when you try to leave Peru. I suggest that you and your daughter stop at the Peruvian immigration office in Lima and get proper stamps in your passports. Until you do, you are here illegally.

"I have no further questions for you at this time. Is there anything else you want to tell me?"

"No," Julia replied, softly and timidly, feeling chastened and uncomfortable.

"You may go now." Ruiz looked at his list of the guests. "Please ask *Señor* Ricardo Dawson to come upstairs next."

Richard sat in the chair facing Ruiz. "I'll tell you anything I can," he said, "but I know nothing about any of the other people here. Except Rosa Mamani, of course."

"You two are novios?"

"Well, sort of. Not officially—at least not yet—but I expect to ask her father when we get back to La Paz. That's what one does here, isn't it? That's the most proper way to become engaged in America."

"Yes, that's right. But now then, why are you here? Why are you in South America? You have been in Bolivia, I think."

"Yes, that's correct. I am a graduate student working toward a PhD in anthropology. I'm interested in the physical adaptations that the human body makes to living at high altitude. And more than that, in the earlier history of that adaptation. When did it start? The early people came here from Chimu, I understand, down on the seacoast. So they adapted after they migrated here. When is a question. And the bony *restos* (remains) from Tiahuanaco are some of the earliest, so that's why I've been working there."

"And Rosa, your chica—correct?"

Richard ignored the implied definition of his relationship with Rosa. "She is also an anthropology student. At UMSA. Professor Ortega is her mentor as well as my Bolivian overseer for this investigation. She has joined me in this project. She is very smart and a great help to me. We work well together."

"And you are staying together here at Machu Picchu."

"Well, yes."

"*Bueno*. That's all for now. Would you ask *Señorita* Mamani to come to talk with me now?"

Rosa made herself comfortable facing Ruiz. Or as comfortable as this inevitably stressful situation permitted.

"*Buenas tardes, Señorita*. I have some questions for you."

"Of course, Captain, and I'll tell you anything I can. But I only just met Arthur after we came here. And the same for all the other guests. Except Ricardo, of course."

"You and Ricardo. You two are *novios*, engaged?"

"Yes. Well yes but not yet officially. Ricardo must speak to my father. He'll do that when we get back to La Paz."

"And when you are married, you will move to *Los Estados*?"

"I suppose, if that's where his career—and mine—take us. But for now and for the next few years, I think we'll be in Bolivia working at Tiahuanaco."

"Now then, *Señorita*, what impression did you have of *Señor* Arthur Greene?"

"Well, I only met him briefly while we were having pisco

before dinner. He seemed sort of pompous, officious, really not very pleasant nor friendly. I didn't like him. But I didn't kill him!"

"Of course not. I'm not accusing you."

"But I don't think any of the other guests knew him before coming here, so something about him must have frightened someone—a lot, enough to kill him."

"Yes, *Señorita*, and I think cocaine smuggling is involved and somehow provided the motive for the murder. May I ask, are you a cocaine user?"

"No, of course not. Well, I tried sniffing it once at a student party, but I didn't like it, and I've never done it again."

"But many students do.

"Yes, but not me."

"And it is easy to obtain in La Paz?"

"Oh yes. Up behind the cathedral there are many women who sell it. The leaves are spread out on aguayos on the pavement in front of where they are sitting."

"But you have never bought any?"

"No. Never. Not all Bolivians use cocaine, you know. Probably no more Bolivians than Peruvians." Rosa felt she had to get in a last, somehow justifying word with Ruiz.

"That will be all for now, *Señorita*. Would you ask *Señor* Mark Strong to come up here. I will talk to him next."

Mark arrived for his interview. He was concerned and felt threatened. He thought his history of drug use might make him a suspect.

"*Señor* Strong. Thank you for talking with us. You understand we are not accusing you of anything, although someone here must have killed Arthur Greene. But at this stage, we are simply gathering information. Tell me what you did after dinner last night."

"Well, I wasn't feeling well for some reason. So I told my

wife I would go to bed. But I didn't. At least not right away. I stepped outside and talked with Charles. He can confirm that. Then he and I each said we would look at the ruins. We started out together, but went separately to different areas after going through the entrance. Then I didn't see him again—or anyone else, really—as I wandered about. I never did get to the sundial area where Arthur was found. I was tired and not feeling well, as I said, so I came back to the inn and went to bed."

"Did you not see others as you walked about the ruins?"

"No. Well, yes I did. I saw my wife and Julia, but not close by. And, also Richard and Rosa. They were all headed out to the ruins. But as I said, I returned to the inn to go to bed. I had told my wife I was tired, so I expect she knew I would make an early night of it."

"Did any of the others see you return to the inn?"

"No, I guess not." Mark paused. "Do you suspect me? I didn't kill him. I didn't like him, although I hardly knew him. None of us did, I guess—know him or like him. He had this air about him of being superior. No—that's not quite right—of somehow sitting in judgment of us, I guess. And his job was to ferret out casual cocaine importers."

"And are you a casual cocaine user?"

Mark hesitated. Then thought that the truth might out and that it should best come from him. "Not now. Not recently. But in the past, I have been."

"But not recently?"

"Yes, not recently."

"How not recently?"

"Well, in fact, my wife brought me on this trip to get me away from my drug suppliers in New York. But, thanks to her, I'm clean now. I had a good job in New York with lots of opportunities in the banking business. I lost it because of using cocaine. I wound up driving a taxi—the only job I could get—and I got these stupid, ugly tattoos. I know you won't believe this, but I will not go back to cocaine. I'm a strong person. I'm smart. I can make it."

"Thank you, *Señor* Strong. That will be all for now. Please ask your wife to come up to us here."

Downstairs, Mark turned to Harriet, "It's your turn. I guess."

"How was it? Bad? Uncomfortable?"

"No. Just some questions. I guess maybe they'll probe deeper, get tougher, if this first questioning doesn't turn up anything."

"Well, it won't, will it? Whoever did this is hardly likely to confess."

"Yeah. But I didn't do it, and I don't think you did. So go up and talk to them."

Harriet led Mark aside as she moved toward the stairs. "Did they ask you about your drug use?"

"Yes, and I admitted it, but I told them I am now clean." Then he added, "I want to quit. I don't ever want to be hooked on drugs again. And I guess that's a large part of why we're on this trip—why you brought me here, far away from New York."

"Yeah. Exactly. And I want to do everything I can possibly do to keep you clean."

"Yes, Harriet. I know you will. And I love you for that. Now, go up there and talk to the policeman."

Harriet went up to the interview room and returned Captain Ruiz's greeting. "I'll tell you everything I can," she said, "but I really don't know much."

"Of course, *Señora*, but as we talk to each of you we hope to understand what might have led to this unfortunate murder. *Entonces*, well then, how well did you know *Señor* Greene, and why do you think someone killed him?"

"Well, I didn't know him—before meeting him here, that is. And I don't think anyone here did. None of us knew each other, except couples, of course. I can't imagine anyone having a reason to kill him, unless it had something to do with cocaine. But I don't think anyone here is in the cocaine business. But some may have been casual users. My husband is—was. Did he tell you that?"

"He did, and said he would stop. But that is difficult, you know."

"Yes, I know. But he is a strong person, and I will help him. It was really bad for him. Cost him his job, a good job. And that's a big part of why we're here. I arranged this trip to get him away, although I didn't realize I was booking us into the heart of cocaine-growing country."

"You and *Señora* Young walked out in the ruins last evening, I understand."

"Yes."

"Did others go out there in the evening? Did you see or meet any of the other inn guests there?"

"No. But we were talking—just chatting—and we weren't paying attention to things. There might have been others out in the ruins. I suppose there probably were. Rosa and Richard, I think, at least. Not much point of staying inside. It was a nice evening, and the reason we all came here was to see the ruins."

"I see. *Claro.* Now then, did you or your husband or any of the others have any difficulties with *Señor* Greene? Can you think of why anyone might have wanted to kill him?"

"Well, obviously, someone did. But I don't know why. Mr. Hewes and he had some words over a small figure that Mr. Hewes stole from a museum, but not enough to lead to murder. I just can't imagine anyone here as a murderer. Nor can I see anyone with a motive. Some may not have liked him, I suppose. But murder…"

"Perhaps I should talk to *Señor* Hewes next. You said he stole a figure from a museum?"

"Yes. He was quite open about it? It made all of us sort of uncomfortable. It's not something American tourists should do, I guess. And, I guess, Arthur seemed quite critical of him."

"I thank you for speaking with me and being so willing to talk about this unfortunate event. Do you have questions for me?"

"No. I think not. But it is hard to realize that someone here is a murderer."

"Of course, and I assure you we will find out who it is."

Ted Hewes sat down opposite Captain Ruiz. "This is a terrible business, and I'll tell you anything I can. I have some thoughts about it."

"No," Ruiz interrupted. "Let me ask you some questions, and then I'll hear your thoughts. "What led you to come to Peru and Machu Picchu at Christmas? Shouldn't you be at home with family?"

"Well, maybe, but no. I'm divorced. If anything, I want to be away from family at holiday times. Those are the hardest times for me."

"Yes, I can understand that. But why here? Why Machu Picchu?"

"Well, I guess there's a story behind that. You see, I served in the Peace Corps in Bolivia. We were introducing hybrid potatoes to Altiplano *campesinos*. Charles Martin, one of the other guests here now, and I. And of course, I learned Spanish. So if I wanted to get away, South America seemed like a good place to go— because I could speak the language. Even though I spent nearly three years just next door, I had never been here. So, I thought it might be a good place to spend the holiday."

"You knew *Señor* Martin?"

"Yes, but I had not seen him in many years. I was surprised to find him here."

"I understand you stole a gold figure from the Museo do Oro in Lima."

"Yes, I did. I should not have. I should get it back. If I give it to you, can you see that it is returned?"

"No, *Señor*. You will have to take it back or give it to the police in Lima. The museum and the Lima police will not look kindly upon you, but if you are caught with it at customs you are likely to wind up in jail.

"Now then, what do you know of the other guests here? Do you think any of them might have had a reason to commit murder. You told me you knew Señor Martin."

"Yes, I did, many years ago. He and I were in Bolivia together, as I said. I also knew Julia Young, although I haven't seen her in many years. She and I were in university together. That was a long time ago, and I hadn't seen her since, until now. I was surprised to meet her and her daughter here.

"I can't say anything about the other people here. Martin and Julia Young are the only ones I knew, and it's been many years for both of them. As I said, Charles Martin and I were together in Bolivia with the Peace Corps, and Julia Young and I were university students together."

"And Martin, could he be the murderer? Or Señora Young?"

"Well, not Julia Young. That just doesn't seem possible to me. But I suppose, if anyone, maybe Charles Martin. I don't know why he would do it. However, he does speak Spanish, and he knows about the Andean region. Maybe he has some involvement in cocaine trade, I suppose. But that's just speculation, a guess. But, but…"

"But what?" Ruiz asked.

"Well, why would he or anyone want to kill Arthur? He told us all that he worked with the American Drug Enforcement Agency to stop cocaine smuggling. And in particular he was currently focused on tourists smuggling cocaine back through customs. I guess that could be any of us, but it must be someone or some persons who could get the cocaine in the first place. And among those of us here, that could only be Charles Martin, I think. Or me, maybe, and I didn't do it. I'm not suggesting that Charles was the murderer, but it seems to me he might have had a motive that the rest of us didn't have. And more than that, the language fluency needed to deal with local *cocaineros*. It's not my place to judge, of course, but it seems to me he's the only one here who had—well, might have had—a motive to kill Arthur Greene."

"Thank you, *Señor* Hewes. You have been most helpful. I think I would now like to talk to the Swedish couple. Would you ask *Señora* Marta Bergstrom to come upstairs, please."

Ruiz greeted Marta and then began the interview. "It would be easier, *Señora*, if you told me the truth about who you are and what you do at the Swedish embassy. I see from your passport that you are actually a Russian citizen. I don't know why the Swedish embassy would hire a Russian, so perhaps you would be kind enough to tell me."

This opening to the interview disturbed Marta. How much could this Ollantaytambo police officer know about embassies and international politics, she wondered. She would tell the truth, or some of it, she decided. But not reveal her espionage work.

"Well," Marta replied, "I was working in a bank and my husband in a travel agency. He found out about Peru, and suggested we might like it here. We talked about it, and in the end we came here. We needed jobs, and played on our Swedish language and background to get work at the Swedish embassy. But we're not diplomats. I'm a housekeeper and my husband is a driver."

"There is more to your story," Ruiz replied. "You could not afford to stay at this inn on the salaries of the positions you say you have. And embassies in Lima hire local drivers and housekeepers.

I can and will find out about you, but it would be easier if you simply told me the truth."

"But I have nothing more to tell you." Marta was uncertain about how to handle this conversation, but she felt that saying more might lead to trouble. Saying nothing—or as little as possible—seemed the best course to her.

"Come with me, *Señora*." Ruiz led her to an adjoining room. He then descended to the inn's foyer and asked Olaf Bergstrom to come upstairs. Thus, he prevented the wife from communicating with her husband.

"Now then, *Señor* Bergstrom. I understand that you are employed as a driver at the Swedish embassy."

"Yes, that is correct."

"So tell me the rest of that story. Surely you did not leave Sweden to come to Peru to be a driver."

"Well, that's it. I learned about Peru because I had a job at a tourist agency. Marta and I thought it would be a good place to be. So we came here and found what work we could at the Swedish embassy."

"Is there more you want to tell me about that?"

"No. That's all there was to it."

"And your job as a driver provided a sufficient salary for you to be able to afford staying at this inn?"

"Well, yes. With both of our salaries. And we saved our money."

Ruiz changed his line of questioning. "Did you know *Señor* Greene in Lima?"

"No. We met him here."

"Are you and your wife cocaine users?"

"No, not really. Well, we have tried it. But not often and not regularly."

"Cocaine is addicting. You were able to use it just occasionally?"

"Yes. Neither of us became addicted to it."

"Have you any thoughts about who might have wanted to murder *Señor* Greene.

"No. He was annoying in his manner, but no more so than many people. Certainly not enough to make me or anyone want to murder him. He did not seem to me to have any major conflict with any of us."

"Yes, of course, but he was also trying to uncover illegitimate cocaine traffic. Have you or your wife been involved in that?"

"No, of course not."

"You are not exploiting your embassy positions to export cocaine?"

"No, never. We're not really embassy people. We just have ordinary jobs there."

"That will be all for now, then. Your wife is in the next room. You may both go downstairs. Please ask Charles Martin to come up to talk with me. He's the only one I have not yet interviewed."

"*Señor* Martin," Ruiz began the last of his interviews with the inn guests, "I understand that you know something of this region."

"Well, a little, but not this part, here. I was in Bolivia years ago with the American Peace Corps. On the Altiplano. Along with *Señor* Hewes."

"And you speak Spanish?"

"*Si. Más o menos.*"

"You walked here from Cuzco, I understand."

"Yes. I'm reasonably fit, and I took three days in Cuzco to adjust to the altitude. It was a pretty good trail and a beautiful walk. I was surprised that I met nobody on the trail. The holiday, I suppose."

"And what is your occupation in North America?"

"I'm a school teacher. In a high school—a *colegio*."

"When we searched your room, we noted some coca leaves. Are you a cocaine user?"

"No. I picked up the coca in Cuzco to chew to help adjust to the altitude. Especially since I was going to walk the trail here and not really rest long enough to become totally adjusted to the altitude. I learned to do that in Bolivia. And I suppose Peruvians do it also."

"Yes, it helps with *soroche*. But you say you are not otherwise a cocaine user?"

"Correct."

"And while on the Altiplano in Bolivia?"

"Not then. And not back home in the 'States.'"

"Now then, *Señor* Martin, can you suggest why any of your fellow guests here might have wished to kill *Señor* Greene?"

"No, I really cannot. None of us knew him before. He was annoying in his manner, but not so much so that someone would murder him. I sat next to him at dinner. He seemed like just an ordinary person to me. A bit shy, perhaps.

"Of course, he told us all that his embassy job was trying to stop cocaine traffic. And more than that, he was looking into cocaine smuggling by tourists. I guess, any one of us could be planning to do that—to take home a bit of cocaine hidden in luggage. But even so, that would hardly seem to be enough of a motive to commit murder."

"True. But suppose you were caught smuggling cocaine. What would that mean to you? Perhaps your embassy would have gotten you out of jail. It's not such a major crime, after all. But what would it mean to your life in the States? Your job? Your ability to continue a career as a teacher? Your friendships? Would not even a rumor that you were a drug user greatly affect your life? No, *Señor* Martin. This cocaine business is terrible and it certainly can provide motives for murder."

Guest interviews concluded, Ruiz descended to the main floor and sought out Fernando, finding him in the kitchen. "I have talked with all of your guests, and I would like to have a few words with you."

"Of course. But I did not know any of them before they arrived here. Nor *Señor* Greene."

"I understand, but you may have made observations that seemed unimportant at the time, but might be helpful. Would you come upstairs with me?"

With the two men comfortably seated, Ruiz reviewed Fernando's employment at the inn and his past employment in Lima. He then said, "You must have many guests here from many countries. Many types of people."

"Yes, we do. Many types. Many different people from different places and of different sorts."

"And so, in your experience, how do the present guests seem to you? Are any of them different in any way? Could any of them have known *Señor* Greene previously? And could any of them be smuggling cocaine, since that seems somehow to be at the heart of this affair."

"*Bueno*, as I said, we get many kinds of guests. Of the present company, only Charles Martin seems a little unusual."

"Oh? Why?"

"Well, he walked here. Those who walk the trail from Cuzco are not usually persons who can afford to stay here in the inn. They usually camp out along the trail and only come to visit the ruins during the day."

"Yes, that must be so. Certainly. I may tell you that we found some coca leaves in *Señor* Martin's room. He said he acquired it in Cuzco to chew while walking the trail, because he was not totally adjusted to the altitude."

"That is logical, I suppose. And I understand that he lived

previously in Bolivia, so he probably learned to chew coca leaves there."

"Yes. Now let me ask you, have you become involved in any way in cocaine traffic? We know, and you probably also know, that Ollantaytambo is home to a number of *cocaineros*. You must know of them. Have you become involved in any even minor way in cocaine traffic?"

"Oh, no! I wouldn't do that. I couldn't. If I did, and if it were discovered, I would lose my job."

"And wind up in jail."

"Yes. I have stayed far away from the cocaine traffic."

"You will all remain here tonight and tomorrow," Ruiz addressed the group after concluding his interview with Fernando. "I will return in the morning and perhaps have more questions and information for you. Meanwhile, enjoy this inn and the ruins, but do not leave. I am sure Fernando will take good care of you."

CHAPTER ELEVEN

An Arrest

FERNANDO REFILLED COFFEE CUPS, moving from person to person. The ten inn guests had spontaneously gathered in the lounge and found seats. It had rained during the night, but the cloudless morning appeared to promise a pleasant, rain-free day. A good day to explore the ruins, perhaps. But wandering about the ruins would wait until after Captain Ruiz's promised morning return.

There was little conversation. Although the murder and Ruiz's assessment of it were uppermost in the minds of all of the guests, none of them wanted to talk about it. One of them was a murderer. None of them wanted to reveal whom he or she suspected. Yet each of them had a private, unspoken opinion. And all of them were apprehensive, knowing that one of them could be violent.

Fernando was walking from the lounge through the front hall to refill his coffeepot, when the front door opened and Captain Ruiz entered. Fernando paused and waited in the hall as Ruiz entered the lounge.

"Good morning," Ruiz said. "I see you are all here. I talked with each of you yesterday. Since then I have communicated with police and security officers in Cuzco and Lima. I have come to some tentative conclusions, but there are some gaps in the information I have and some questions that need additional answers. Thus, I'm afraid I'm going to ask each of you to talk with me again. For some of you, I will have only a few points to clarify. For others, more probing questions, perhaps.

"Fernando," Ruiz said addressing the inn's manager, "This investigation will require the inn to be closed today. The buses will be running again, but we have put up signs to tell all visitors that there will be no luncheon served at the inn today. And we have told the bus drivers. Officer Martinez is erecting a sign outside the inn and a cordon of yellow tape to keep people away. The ruins will be open, although some of the areas related to the murder will be closed and cordoned off. Additional officers will be stationed there.

"Now then, *entonces,*" Ruiz addressed the group. "I will talk with each of you individually, just as I did yesterday. Then I would like each of you with whom I have talked to find a place away from the others. There should be no communication between those whom I have interviewed and those whom I have not yet seen today. That is normal procedure in an investigation of this sort. Perhaps those with whom I have talked can use the dining room or porch, while the others stay here in the lounge. Will that work satisfactorily, Fernando?"

"Yes, of course, and we can serve lunch both here and on the porch."

"*Bueno, Señorita* Erica Young. I would like to start with you, as I did yesterday. Please come upstairs with me.

Erica followed Ruiz to the second floor interview room. Nervous, perhaps apprehensive, not knowing what to expect or what might be expected of her, she took a seat in the chair opposite the table where Captain Ruiz sat. Ruiz sat quietly, saying nothing, and that made her even more anxious.

"I told you everything I know yesterday."

"You were the person who found *Señor* Greene with a knife in his chest."

"Yes."

"And the knife penetrated his heart? And killed him?"

"Yes, I guess, I suppose so."

"And was there much blood?"

"No, I don't think so. I don't remember blood."

"Didn't that surprise you? No, let me withdraw that question. You probably were not in a frame of mind where you would have thought about that at the time. But let me tell you, there was no blood."

"Shouldn't there have been? I mean, he was stabbed in the heart."

"Suppose I tell you that he was killed elsewhere and then carried to the stone where you found him?"

"Is that what happened? Then there would be blood elsewhere, wouldn't there be?"

"Perhaps. But we have not found blood any other place."

"But..." Erica paused, apparently thinking. Watching her carefully during this discussion, Ruiz had become convinced that she did not know more details of the murder and that he need not consider her as a suspect in the killing. "But, if you think he was stabbed someplace else and then carried to the place where I found him, shouldn't there be blood where he was murdered?"

"*Señorita*, he was already dead when he was stabbed."

"What! Then how..."

"How was he killed?"

"Yes."

"He was garroted."

"Garroted? What's that?"

"The murderer put this piece of rope around his neck and twisted it tight to kill him." Ruiz pulled a piece of rope about two feet long from his pocket. "We found this rope on the ground near a trash can beside the inn's kitchen door."

"Oh, my! So then why the knife?"

"Only the murderer knows that, of course, but I suspect it was to dramatize the killing. To make a statement to someone or some persons."

"Oh, but this is confusing. I don't understand."

"Yes, but we will figure it out. You and the other guests can be sure of that. I have no more questions for you. Do you have anything else you want to tell me or ask me?"

"No. No, I can't think of any other questions."

"Good, I will walk downstairs with you and escort you to the porch. Officer Martinez will be there with you. Please do not make any attempt to talk to any of the others." Ruiz rose, offered a gracious hand to Erica as she rose, and escorted her down to the porch.

"*Señora* Julia Young, I would like to talk with you now." Julia rose and followed Ruiz to the interview room. Somehow she was nervous, although she was not sure why. She sat down in the chair opposite Ruiz, smoothing her slacks. She brushed her hair back from her face with her hand.

"*Señora*, you work in a travel agency in New York, correct?"

"Yes, I told you that yesterday."

"And you book airline flights for *cocaineros*—cocaine smugglers."

"What?" Julia was disturbed by this question. How much did Ruiz know? How much could he know?

"My colleagues in Lima have told me that your travel agency has come to their attention in this regard."

"Well, I don't know. We sell airline tickets to anyone who comes into the office and can pay for the ticket. But most of our business is from regular clients whose credit cards we have on file. Mostly business people. If some of them smuggle cocaine, we don't know of it. How would we?" This line of questioning disturbed Julia. How much did Ruiz know? Could he have learned that she regularly and knowingly booked flights for cocaine traffickers?

"Let me ask you more about the murder." Ruiz pulled the garrote from his pocket. "Do you know what this is?"

"A rope, isn't it?"

"Yes, and in this case a garrote."

"A garrote? What's that?"

"A rope used for strangling. And in this instance for strangling *Señor* Greene."

"But he was stabbed. We saw the knife."

"Yes, but he was dead when he was stabbed."

"I don't understand."

"Neither do we, *Señora*, but we will find out.

"I have no further questions for you now. Do you want to ask me anything more?"

"No, I guess not."

"*Bueno*. I will walk downstairs with you. You will wait with your daughter, but not talk to the others at this time."

Ruiz next questioned Harriet and Mark, Richard and Rosa, and then Marta and Olaf. As he had with the Youngs, mother and daughter, he reviewed their stories with them individually. He pressed each of them about cocaine use and trafficking. He presented the garrote rope to each of them, and sensed that they each were genuinely surprised that it had been used to murder Arthur Greene. Probably not the murderer, he concluded about each of them, although each of them probably had reason to be concerned about Arthur Greene's interest in individual cocaine users and smugglers.

Ruiz next questioned Charles. "*Señor* Martin, you are a cocaine user," Ruiz began.

"No. Why do you think I might be?"

"But we found coca leaves in your room."

"Yes, I told you I bought that in Cuzco to help with the altitude as I walked here."

"Do you expect me to believe that? Do you expect me to believe that you bought coca leaves just for your walk?"

"Well, it's the truth."

Ruiz then produced the garrote and questioned Charles about it. Once again, he felt that Charles did not recognize the rope, although as with the others concealing recognition would not have been difficult.

Ruiz's final interview of the morning was with Ted Hewes. He retraced the earlier conversation he had had with Hewes and then abruptly asked, "You implicated *Señor* Martin. Why?"

"Well, I don't know. I guess trying to solve this murder is not really my job. But I can't help thinking about it. I guess you've figured out how it was done, and any one of us could have put that rope around Arthur's neck. So in my mind it comes down to 'why?' And somehow I've come to think that cocaine use probably provided the motive. And Charles Martin told us all he had purchased cocaine or at least coca leaves, in Cuzco."

"We also believe that cocaine use and trafficking in the drug might have provided the motive. And that casts its shadow on all of you except the young woman, Erica Young, and probably also the couple, Rosa Mamani and Richard Dawson. Including you, I believe. Are you a cocaine user?"

"No, never."

"You do a great deal of business in Latin America, including Peru…"

"Yes, but legitimate investments."

"Not importing cocaine to North America?"

"No. No."

"Do you have anything else you want to tell me? Or questions?"

"No," Ted replied, feeling relieved, but humbled.

Descending to the first floor, Ruiz and Hewes were greeted by Fernando. Lunch is ready, Captain. Humberto and I will serve it in the dining room."

"Is there a small, private room where Officer Martinez and I can eat while we review our findings?"

"Of course."

"Perhaps there is a room with a telephone. I may wish to call Lima again."

"No problem."

While the guests lunched, Ruiz and Martinez reviewed their findings. They made phone calls both to Cuzco and Lima.

Following lunch, Ruiz addressed the ten guests who had gathered in the lounge. "I am sure you are all anxious to hear the results of our investigation. Let me begin by noting what must be obvious to all of you. There are ten of you, and one of you must have murdered Arthur Greene. Well, perhaps I should also include Fernando and Humberto, the cook. But they are not serious suspects. Any one of you might have had the opportunity to commit this crime. Therefore I have had to ask myself 'why would one of you have done it? What could have been the motive?'

"After talking with each of you, I am convinced that cocaine smuggling is behind the killer's actions. And most of you are occasional cocaine users. Not the usual cocaine traffickers that we in Peru and the American DEA agents are so often concerned about. But Arthur Greene made it apparent to all of you that he was interested in pursuing casual cocaine smugglers. People such as any one of you might be. People seeking to get through immigration and customs with just a little cocaine for personal use, perhaps. And, more seriously, people seeking to establish communications, relationships, and potential routes for future smuggling activities. Could this be a serious motive for a murder? Unfortunately, yes. Cocaine is an addicting drug, and the actions of addicts and persons who supply drugs to addicts are hard to understand for innocent non-users.

"There are other aspects of any possible perpetrator to consider. Of some importance is the question of how and where a cocaine smuggler might obtain the drug he or she planned to smuggle. Unfortunately, that is not difficult in most of Peru. Certainly it is easy in Cuzco, through which all of you passed. However, most tourists do not come in contact with cocaine traffickers in Cuzco or elsewhere. And fluency in Spanish is important in this regard."

None of the guests spoke or interrupted Ruiz. His comments were apt, but also disquieting.

Ruiz paused. He looked around the room, seemingly assessing each person. Then he spoke. "*Señor* Charles Martin, will you stand, please." Martin rose slowly. "*Señor* Martin, I arrest you on suspicion of the murder of Arthur Greene. Officer Pérez and I will take you to Ollantaytambo now. After the New Year you will be taken to Cuzco to appear before a magistrate and then tried by judges for the murder of Arthur Greene."

"But I didn't… I'm innocent. I'm not guilty. I didn't do it."

"You will have an opportunity to plead before judges according to the laws of Peru. But I advise you to be careful and perhaps say nothing more at this time."

"But I didn't do it! I'm innocent."

Epilogue

"PUT DOWN THE GUN, Charles." Ted rose to his feet and moved across his office away from his desk and towards Charles. "I may not have always been an exemplary citizen, but I am not a murderer. I did not kill that man in Machu Picchu. You are wrong."

"Oh, yes you did." The gun wavered in Charles' hand. "I've had years and years to think this through. Cocaine was at the center of all that went on, including the murder. There were ten of us. We were all at least casual cocaine users. But someone had to have more than a casual acquaintance with the drug to be motivated to murder. Someone was probably making a lot of money smuggling it into the States. And you are the only one who could have been doing that. You with all of your international business connections."

"No, Charles. I didn't do it." Ted walked slowly toward Charles. He reached out and took the gun from his hand. Charles let it go easily, glad to do so, it seemed. Ted put it on the desk where it could not be quickly reached.

"Sit down, Charles. I pretty much put the whole thing out of my mind years ago, and I haven't thought about it much since. But maybe I should have. Maybe we should—together, now."

The two men sat in side chairs, a low table between them. Ted said, "Okay, so there were ten of us, and if we leave the two of us out, that brings it down to eight. None of them seem obvious killers to me, so I think we have to ask what might have been the motive."

"Yes," Charles commented. "That's just how I have tried to think about this—over and over again while sitting in a dirty jail cell. And I think that cocaine use and smuggling were at the heart of it. And, I believe, you are the only one of us who could set up and hide a cocaine trafficking operation. You are fluent in Spanish and know the Andean culture—or at least you once did. Not so for most of the others."

"Right. I'm sure you're right that cocaine smuggling provided the motive. But it was not me. I am not a drug trafficker. So then, the question is who? Who was so much involved with cocaine traffic as to become a murderer? You decided it was me, but it was not. I do a lot of international finance, but I have never been involved in drug smuggling."

"Well, I've thought about that. About who. For twenty years."

"I'm sure you have."

"So, first there were the woman and her daughter, Julia and Erica. Julia was a bit unconventional, eccentric, perhaps. Erica a good woman; I liked her. I don't see either of them as having a motive, and Erica certainly would not have burst in upon us with the news she had discovered Arthur's body—unless that was part of a major act. But I don't think so. I wonder what has happened to that young woman. Smart and attractive."

"Charles, I guess I should tell you. Julia and I were in college together. We had an affair. Erica is my daughter, although she

doesn't know it. I have kept track of her. She is now married. She
and her husband own a small resort in Northern Minnesota. You
can read about them on the Internet; their resort has a website.
They've just installed a zip line, whatever that is. "

"Well, how about that! Then the Swedish couple. Or Russian.
Or whatever they were. I don't see them as having a motive, and
I think that Peruvian law would have caught up with them if they
were felons. Actually, I think they were not the diplomats we all
assumed they were. Just low-level embassy employees. And the
couple from New York. He had all those tattoos. They were on
vacation. That seems odd, because I would have thought that
their Christmas vacation would have been spent with family. I
guess all of those four were casual drug users. Finally there were
the young couple, she Bolivian, he American. They were working on an archeology project of some sort. Maybe casual cocaine
users, maybe not. But when I thought about all of them, all eight
of them, none of them seemed like possible murderers. None
had a motive."

"Charles, I've long since put this whole business out of my
mind, but I think I agree with what you are saying now. It seems
to me that cocaine was at the heart of it. Whoever killed Arthur
did it because he or she was a drug trafficker, and the risk of being
exposed by Arthur as a *cocainero* must have been the motive for
the murder. But there's more to think about. If cocaine traffic
provided the motive, the murderer must also have had contact
with local suppliers, maybe in Ollantaytambo, and must have
been fluent in Spanish. None of the other guests could have had
that contact—nor could even have mustered enough Spanish for
it. Possibly the young anthropology or archeology couple. They
spoke Spanish. But I just don't— can't—see them as murderers."

"So," Charles continued, "that leaves you and me. None of
the others fit, and I know I did not do it."

DEATH COMES TO MACHU PICCHU

"Nor did I. I didn't do it. Really. Believe me, Charles, I did not kill Arthur."

"Then who?"

The two men sat still, looking at each other. An eternity-seeming minute or two passed. "FERNANDO!"

Author's Note

This novel is a work of fiction. All of the characters are fictional and bear no relation to any person or persons known to me. The narrative is entirely of my imagination.

The settings for this work are actual places in Peru, and I have visited all of them, from Salaverry to Lima, from Cuzco to Machu Picchu. I have stayed at the inn at Machu Picchu three times, the last in 1985. I have described it as I remember it, with some modifications to facilitate the course of my story. However, my research has told me that the inn has changed and that accommodations there are no longer available. The ruins, of course, are immutable.

My wife, Janet, has supported me in many ways as I have immersed myself in writing this book. She also accompanied me on my three trips to Machu Picchu, as she has on many of my other travels in Latin America. I am also grateful to my daughter, Ginnie, who read my manuscript and made helpful suggestions. She has been to Machu Picchu with me twice.